advance praise for
CRADLE AND GRAVE

"Anya Ow gives us a hallucinatory fever dream that entices the reader to puzzle out its many alien facets and a setting grounded firmly in deep characters and lived-in world building. *Cradle and Grave* is a tour de force of astounding body horror and a heartbreaking transhuman narrative. It is simply perfect."
—Jordan Shiveley, *Dread Singles*

"Anya Ow's *Cradle and Grave* is a taunt, stunningly imaginative addition to post-apocalyptic literature. I was hooked from page one by Lien and a world that walks the fine line between body horror and biopunk with ease. Ow has an incredible talent for descriptions that draw an entire picture in just a few words, be it of the monsters that hunt the protagonists on their journey or a tender relationship."
—Lina Rather, author of *Sisters of the Vast Black*

"Get in, losers, we're going to the Scab! The imaginative, climate-devastated world of *Cradle & Grave* drives you forward on a *Fury Road* cutting through *Annihilation*'s Area X."
—K.M. Szpara, author of *Docile*

Neon Hemlock Press
www.neonhemlock.com
@neonhemlock

Cradle and Grave
Anya Ow

Cover Illustration by Y.C. Yang
Cover Design by dave ring

ISBN-13: 978-1-952086-02-1

Anya Ow
CRADLE AND GRAVE

Neon Hemlock Press

THE 2020 NEON HEMLOCK NOVELLA SERIES

Cradle and Grave

BY ANYA OW

To my mother, Leelin, for being an inspiration and for always encouraging my love of books, and to my friends and family, for being there for me over the years.

CHAPTER ONE

Dar Lien died when she was two years and three days old.
The memory wasn't worth much this close to the Scab.
To stay afloat, Lien kept her nose clean and served Changed
and prefabs alike between supply runs. Tael was tael. It was hard
enough eking out a decent living in Basa'at without worrying
over whose skin was vat-grown. As such, when the prefab halfer
trotted up under the tattered awning of her provision shop and
pretended to inspect Lien's selection of water containers, Lien
smiled and uncurled her multi-jointed sets of legs from under her
belly. She pulled herself off the cot behind her desk, picking her
way past wire racks of gewgaws and trinkets.

"Genuine pre-tech. Found most of those myself. Out in the
Scab."

The halfer looked unimpressed by Lien's sales pitch.
Disappointing start. From the waist up, they looked fully
humanoid. No visible blemishes. Sleek muscular torso and long
arms, swaddled in a worn black bomber jacket buttoned over
dull black shell armour. Recon gear, maybe from the Jinsha'an
foundries. They wore heavy brass goggles, and the rest of their
brown face was covered by a discoloured grey scarf and the wide
brim of a straw hat. Holstered at their waist was a combat knife.

"You do sup runs?" the halfer asked in a low monotone. The
halfer's horselike half shifted their weight restlessly on plate-sized
hooves, their charcoal grey pelt dusty and travel-stained. The
tail had been cut into a bob, and it twitched as the halfer ambled
closer. They towered two full hands above her.

"Sure. Three times a year, over into the Scab." Her own knives were close at hand. Dangling in their scabbards by the door.

"By yourself?"

"No one's that reckless unless they're tired of living."

"When's the next run?"

"Three months, maybe. But I'll tell you straight off, stranger. The only sup run worth going on is Raahi's. And Raahi doesn't like prefabs."

The halfer tensed. "Fighting words."

"You've tried to hide the fact that you're a halfer with the spikes. People who got warped by Change don't have mutations that regular. If I've noticed, other people 'round these parts will too. Sooner or later. Basa'at's none too prefab friendly. Buy what you can and shove off if you don't want trouble."

"I'd like to hire a guide. Into the Scab." The halfer made a show of looking around the shop. "Deposit up front. Rest on return."

Lien shook her head, folding both her front limbs and the jointed vestigial spines at her flank. "I'll only go on a run if Raahi's leading it. Are you gonna buy something or not?"

"Not yet," the halfer said. They took a worn envelope from a pocket in their jacket, handing it over. "My employer and I have rooms in the Worker's. You change your mind, look for me. We'll be in town for another couple of days."

"Don't hold your breath," Lien said, irritated by the presumption. The halfer tipped their straw hat and wheeled out of the shop. Steel-shod hooves thudded on the dirt road beyond, driving up small clouds of dust into her shop. Asshole.

Grumbling under her breath, Lien minced back to her cot and heaved herself onto it, the patched leather creaking under her weight. She considered tossing the envelope aside, turning it over and over in her translucent claws. Lien knew bait when she saw it, but her curiosity soon eked out a narrow win over her caution. She sliced it open with a flick of her nail.

Lien hadn't known what to expect. A letter, perhaps. A bribe. Not a single photograph, an old colourstat. It was crinkled at the edges, the colours long faded and murky. Didn't matter. Changer's balls, the subject was clear enough. It'd only been thirty-five years since she'd died. The Room was the last—or the first—thing that Lien remembered.

The halfer didn't react at all when Lien pulled herself up onto the stool opposite them in the paddock half of the Worker's.

Lien scowled. "How did you get your hands on that photo?"

"Got resources."

"What kind of resources?" Lien asked. The halfer stared at her. It wasn't a friendly look. Lien pressed on. "You're from out of town. There are better scouts out there."

"Few as experienced with the Scab."

"Don't give me that 'experienced' shit. I've told you that I only do Raahi runs. Best-resourced, researched runs out there. Without him and his team, 'experience' counts for balls."

The halfer glanced around, checking for listeners. The Worker's was quiet this time of year off the trade season. They were the only people in the paddock. The indoor half had only a couple of people, tucked in a corner and nursing rotgut jugs. The halfer's tail twitched as they lowered their voice. "We want to go to the City. Heard that you survived a return trip. Alone."

Lien pursed her lips. "I didn't go in by myself. If you heard that story, then you know that no one else came back but me."

"We know the risk."

"How many taels are we talking here?"

"Five thousand up front. Ten when we reach the City."

Despite herself, Lien whistled low under her breath. "Fifteen thousand taels could buy you into a run led by Raahi himself. Even with his dislike of prefabs."

"Raahi isn't here."

Lien hadn't survived this long out on the edge of the Scab without being stupid, but damn the Changer, she was tempted. Five thousand taels could buy her way East into the Quarantined Cities. It could buy her the best surgery there was on any market. Swap out her Changed jointed legs, her insectile-jointed thorax and belly—her souvenirs from an early Scab run gone sour. Money like that could freeze the Change before it reached her brain with an Injunct. Five thousand taels would save her life.

And besides. The *photograph*. Even knowing that it was in her pocket sent a chill up her warped spine. "Okay. I'll do it."

The halfer stretched out a hand, the palm large enough to

engulf the delicate claw of Lien's right hand. "Yusuf. Pronouns are he/him."

Lien hadn't been able to place his accent. Now she tried to place his name. "I use she/her. Where are you from, Yusuf? Selangor?"

Yusuf ignored the question. "Gather what you need. Leave at first light."

"I want my deposit now."

Yusuf pushed his hand into the pouch bound at his waist and tossed a taelstick over to Lien. The charge was marked full on the slim silver tube, about as wide as her clawed thumb and just as long. The amount was printed along its flank in discreet numbers. "Satisfied?" Yusuf asked.

Lien pocketed the taelstick, trying not to let her breathing hitch in excitement. This was legit, then. This wasn't a dream. "You're going to need water purif pills," Lien said briskly. "Preferably two or three per day, per person. Bring three weeks' worth. I've got my own. There's plenty of water in the Scab, but none of it's drinkable as is. As to food, there's a fair chance that there's nothing edible out in the Scab at this time of year. Nothing safe. I'll bring my own rations. You two bring yours."

"Don't worry about us."

"I'm serious. This is going to be nothing like you've ever been through before. Scab's ground zero for the Change. You think going through the Scablands was bad? Compared to the Scab, it's light exercise. You're paying me to guide you to the City. I'm not going to babysit you or your 'employer'."

"Don't worry about us," Yusuf repeated, tipping his hat. "See you in the morning. At your provision shop."

A veteran of Scab runs, Lien packed from habit. She triple-checked her supplies, closed down the shop, then rested, trying not to think on the trip ahead. She'd need the sleep.

The sound of hooves woke her up just before first light. Lien stumbled a little blearily out of her provision shop, just in time to see Yusuf come to a stop. Someone was seated on Yusuf's back. The worn saddle was notched between two of his spines, cinched neatly under his belly. The horse blanket was dusty but well-made, patterned intricately under the dirt. A bedroll was strapped down over heavy-looking saddlebags.

Lien had never seen anyone saddle a halfer before. She gawped. Yusuf stared at her, expressionless. "Morning," he said.

"Morning," Lien echoed. Yusuf's rider was wrapped tight in shapeless robes and cloaks. They made no greeting. "I was just about to have a cuppa. Oolong powder. Want some?"

Yusuf shook his head. "Finish up. We'll wait here."

Self-conscious, Lien hurried through breakfast. When she re-emerged, she saw that Yusuf hadn't moved, nor had his rider dismounted. "You're just going to carry your friend through the Scab?"

"My business. Ready?"

"Do I get a name?" Lien gestured at the rider. Yusuf ignored her, starting on a brisk trot towards Basa'at's perimeter.

Lien had to scuttle to keep up. This early in the morning, Basa'at was a ghost town. For once Lien was glad of it. The night's sleep had made her wary of the deal she had signed up on, even though the taelstick had checked out legit. What was she doing? Not even Raahi dared the Scab with anything less than a full dozen crew: spotters, muscle, snifters, techs. A three-person walk wasn't going to cut it.

"Look," Lien said, when she caught up. "I was thinking maybe we should pick up more crew. Three people isn't a good number for the Scab. You clearly have the creds to hire more."

"You made it back through the Scab alone before."

Lien narrowed her eyes, but Yusuf wasn't even looking at her. "I can tell you straight off," she said, with a bitter laugh, "that I did it by following the Rinse to its mouth, where the Change runs so hot that not even the monsters come close, and I paid my due for it, I did."

"Don't worry about the Change," Yusuf said. His confidence shook Lien. She stared hard at Yusuf's silent rider, then at the saddlebags, trying to glean some sort of clue.

Some sort of secret Jinsha'an tech, perhaps? Or a vaccine? The thought of either made her pulse quicken as they stepped past the concrete post that marked the end of Basa'at. The border town of Basa'at perched on a vast intact spur of concrete and metal, a highway ruin that arched over weed-choked roads. Other highway ruins crumbled around them into the Hundred Teeth, smashed out around Basa'at's ridge into long bars of ruined concrete and metal that stretched through barren lands in all directions. A fragment-memory of the world during the Last Summer, before the Change. The sticky air was thick with low-hanging clouds. Wasn't the rainy season, but it rained every week or so in these parts.

Nothing lived in the Hundred Teeth but insects and rats. Lien still peered up now and then into the grey-cloaked sky, with its perpetual dull haze of ash. She was instinctively searching for a hint of great shadows. Scab's Sight, veterans called it. After the Scab, the open sky never felt saf e again.

Multi-jointed legs were good for picking her way through the scree. Lien was concerned about Yusuf at first, but he was sure-footed despite his size. He kept silent until they cleared the Hundred Teeth to the cracked ground that made up the Western Scablands. This outlying sector was a series of canals of oily water and the jagged brick corpses of shophouses, washing up against the walls of refuse in the distance that marked the boundary of the Scab.

"Leads into the Scab," Yusuf said. It wasn't a question.

Lien wasn't sure whether he was talking to her or to his rider. "We'll reach the fringe of the Western Scablands close to the evening. Best make camp on the outskirts and make the crossing in the morning. The Vault's not a kind place in the dark."

"What's the Vault?"

"Underground tunnels. Sewer or storm drains."

"I won't be able to fit. Or climb out if I have to."

"That's the way I'm used to going into the Scab. We'll use the canals that are large enough for sup carts. It'll lead out close to the Mall. Decent rest stop there."

"We go overland," Yusuf said.

"Everything between the Fringe through to the Lake District is psychon territory. We won't make it. They'll probably kill me and your friend. Slowly. You? They'll yoke you to one of their drafts, work you till you're nearly dead. Then they'll eat the four-legged part of you. Cut you into horsey steak."

"Not worried about psychons," Yusuf said. His rider reached over and patted his flank with a heavy glove. Yusuf twisted to glance behind his shoulder. Whatever Yusuf saw under the rider's hood made him scowl. "Fine. Sewers it is."

Lien stared at the rider with renewed interest, but Yusuf had picked up his pace. She had to take longer strides to keep up, to her irritation. They took a break at midday in the hulk of an old building so worn by the dust and weather that Lien couldn't quite pick out its original purpose. Over the years, Raahi and the crew had taken to patching it up until it was now fairly usable as a stopover between outposts. It wasn't stocked with caches, but at least it was out of the sun.

Lien sat down by a brick wall to take a measure of water. She folded her legs carefully under her belly and tried not to stare as Yusuf passed a waterskin to the rider. The rider drank with the hood down. Lien could still get no measure of her silent companion. It worried her, but five thousand taels were five thousand reasons to keep her peace. At least for now.

"You look like you're from the Pyriat," Lien told Yusuf instead, to pass the time as they rested. "Your accent." Yusuf inclined his head. "Which part?"

"Yaran," Yusuf said, naming a town—or city—that Lien had never heard of.

"That where you got the work done?"

"Not all of it," Yusuf said, guarded again.

"It's good work." Lien kept her voice idle. "Might be interested in a bit of a fix myself from a clinic like that."

Yusuf's stare flicked briefly over her, though she couldn't see past his goggles. "Wouldn't do it there. Jinsha'an will have what you need."

"How do you know what I need?"

"You're three-quarters Changed. At least. Need a very thorough Injunct. Maybe a full prefab of the rest. All you can get. In the time you've got."

Lien scowled to cover her unease. She never liked being reminded of how far she was into the Change. Especially by prefabs. "I've got years left yet, halfer."

"Sure," Yusuf said, unimpressed. "It's your life."

This was going to be *such* an entertaining trip. Lien ate her rations in silence. Yusuf and his rider ate what looked like a couple of small energy bars. Jinsha'an make, by their stamps. Raahi had brought a stash during the last Scab run, but it had been unpopular. The bars gave you energy, but they were hardly filling. Worse, they tasted like mouldy cardboard. Lien preferred dried rations any day of the week.

Judging from how slowly the rider was eating, Lien guessed that they weren't enjoying the bars either. On an impulse, she dug into her bag and tossed over a ration pack. "Here. Try this instead."

Lien hadn't expected the rider to startle and flinch. Yusuf snatched the pack out of the air inches before it would have smacked into the rider's shoulder. Too late. The rider had brought up their hands instinctively, causing the heavy cloak to draw back from their frame. Under the cloak, the rider wore a grey leather vest, breeches, and heavy boots. They looked absolutely Unchanged. No lumps under the form-fitting vest. No spurs or strange folds in the breeches, no hint of scales or fur on their bared skin.

Impossible.

"How…?" Lien breathed. Yusuf tensed up and backed a couple of steps, already on the defensive. The rider touched Yusuf lightly on the flank and Yusuf came to a stop, though his weight shifted uneasily between his hooves.

"I suppose this is as good a time as any," the rider said. Their voice was fussy and soft. They drew their hood back to reveal a middle-aged brown face. The rider was clean-shaven, their bright eyes darting a little nervously between Lien and Yusuf. They wore wire-framed lenses over their sharp nose, their small mouth drawn into a thin downward curve. "My apologies for not introducing myself earlier, Miss Dar Lien. I am the one known as Servertu."

It was a strange turn of phrase. "Pleased," Lien said. Servertu's mouth ticked upwards briefly into a mirthless smile at Lien's open insincerity. Yusuf sniffed.

"I use he/him pronouns. What about you?"

"She/her," Lien said. "Call me Lien."

"As to the 'how' of it… you've been engaged to guide us to the City, not ask questions," Servertu said. He pulled his hood over his face again, clouding it in shadow. "I trust that we're paying you enough for your discretion."

It wasn't too late to turn back. But the taels. The Gods-damned Change, so close to destroying her brain. "Guess you are. Five minutes. Then we should get moving."

CHAPTER TWO

They made camp for the day in the safehouse before the Vault, within the ruin of a concrete tiered building from the Last Summer Era. It had been a storage facility for the oily, rusted hulks of ancient machines. Cars, Raahi had called them. He'd told Lien during one of their earliest runs that some of the machines could once fly, that bigger ones had carried hundreds of people across the world within hours. Well-travelled as Raahi was, Lien found that hard to believe.

The building's access was almost all ramp based, making it easy for Yusuf to follow, though the low ceiling meant that his straw hat brushed the cracked surface. He had to hunch down to clear the faded signage. Yusuf's shod hooves made far too much echo against concrete for Lien's comfort. She found herself sneaking nervous glances through the unbroken horizontal openings that spanned the length of each tier above a waist-high barrier, looking out over the Scablands to the east.

Yusuf picked his way to the western side of the building, studying the start of the Scab. The ruined jungle crept to a halt only a couple of hours' walk west, starting with the walls of trash shored up between squat fists of low-lying ruins and rising into the distant fingers of gigantic grey edifices, visible from here as a jagged scrawl against the darkening skyline.

The City.

Servertu dismounted stiffly. Lien flinched in surprise, averting her eyes as Yusuf stared pointedly at her. Servertu ignored them both, stretching and rubbing his back. He ambled towards the barrier, resting his elbows on it and looking out over the Scab.

Yusuf put a hand on Servertu's shoulder. "Not so close. Crows can still get you. Near dark enough out for hunting. Might be close enough to the Scab that they can range out here."

Lien stared at Yusuf appraisingly. He knew about the Crows. Either he was well informed, or he was a veteran himself. Servertu made a dismissive gesture, but he did take a couple of steps back. "How long to the City?"

"Safe going? 'Bout a week to get to the Rinse. Maybe more. And if you're hell-bent on following the Rinse into the City, that'll be a week more," Lien said.

"Is there a faster route?"

"Not running three of us there isn't."

"Told you," Yusuf said. He scraped a hoof on the ground. Servertu glanced at Yusuf and patted one dusty flank, a casual intimacy that was just as odd as the fact that Yusuf had allowed himself to be saddled. Prefabs were usually twitchy. Protective of their prefab parts. Servertu rummaged through the saddlebags, pulling out sleeping gear and a firestarter kit. He unbuckled the saddle and saddlebags, arranging them in a careful pile on the floor.

"No fire," Lien said quickly, "not up here. Crows will see it for miles."

"Ah. Sorry." Servertu stowed the kit back into the bags. "I was hoping to have a quick cup of tea before turning in."

"Have a cup in the morning," Yusuf told him, still eyeing the Scab. "Should be safer. Depending on the light. I'll keep watch."

The week Lien had spent dragging her way out of the Scab had taught her paranoia, a useful trait out on a run. She spent an hour setting up tripwire alarms on the ramp access and on the horizontal openings, handmade systems linked to clappers and tiny bells. Servertu watched her all the while with childlike curiosity, sitting cross-legged beside Yusuf on a neat pile of bedding. Not for the first time that day, Lien wondered who the Changer Servertu was.

When she was done, Servertu asked, "Expecting company?"

Lien settled down on her own bedding. "Doesn't hurt to be careful."

"Crows?"

"Psychons won't come this far out. But sometimes you get the occasional raiders. Rare this close to the Scab, but it's best to be careful. And there's always the ghulkin."

Yusuf studied one of the little clappers attached to a tripwire. "Primitive."

Servertu sighed. "Yusuf."

"Those helped me get out of the Scab alive," Lien said. She wished she didn't sound so defensive. "They work."

"No doubt." Servertu curled on his flank, hugging his arms around his chest with a yawn. "Now, if you'll excuse me. It's been a long day." In only a few breaths, Servertu curled more comfortably on the bedding, out like a light. He was deeply asleep the way no-one sensible should sleep. Not this far west.

Doubt started to worry its way back into Lien. Going into the Scab with just two units was bad enough. Going in with one total rookie was impossible. She cleared her throat, but Yusuf spoke first in a low voice. "Know what you're thinking. Don't worry about us."

"He's UnChanged, isn't he?" Lien asked challengingly. Yusuf turned around to face her. The halfer's hands were loose at his sides, but his hooves planted themselves firmly on the concrete, tail twitching. Tense.

"What about it?"

"You've clearly done this before. Has he?"

Yusuf swallowed a harsh noise, and it took Lien a moment to realize that it was a laugh. "Does it matter?"

"Yeah. If he's no more than a tourist, this isn't going to work."

"Why?"

"Even if you're a Jinsha'an Paladin," Lien growled, "the Scab's dangerous. Babysitting someone who can't fight or take care of themselves is suicide. He can't be paying you enough to do this. Changer, *I'm* not paid enough to do this."

"We'll see," Yusuf said, with his irritating self-confidence.

"Maybe I should get the rest of my pay up front."

"Not until the City," Yusuf countered, then he let out another harsh noise. "Or pick it off our bodies if we die."

"I should turn back."

"Do it then. Five thousand taels won't do you much. Choose

between an Injunct and prefab work."

"Where have you been, eh?" Lien challenged, ignoring Yusuf's baiting. "Bakgut Plains? Subterra? Selangor?"

"Been around. Selangor was a brief stop. Nasty place. Too many ghulkin."

"You're a Paladin."

"Nope."

"Why else would you visit so many sectors of the Changelands? And the prefab job that you've had done is solid stuff. Seamless. I thought only Paladins get that lucky."

"Didn't get this because I was lucky," Yusuf said. He turned to face one of the viewing slats. "Sleep."

Servertu's puttering around woke Lien in the morning. He turned his back politely as Lien crawled somewhere quiet to perform her morning's absolutions, already in a foul mood. It took a while to disable her traps. None had been tripped during the night. Good sign. Bars for breakfast for Servertu and Yusuf, another ration pack for Lien. This time, Lien didn't offer to share.

"Where did you get that photograph?" Lien asked as she opened her ration pack. She tried to keep her tone even, but she could feel the edge creeping into her voice.

Servertu smiled. "I'm an Archivist."

"Meaning?"

"Meaning that I'm privy to a lot of unusual information."

"And?"

"It's said that the first of the Changed recall the moment of their 'deaths'—their infection—with crystal clarity. Whatever age they were at the time."

Lien hesitated. "Is this why you wanted me to come? You want me to find the… the Room?" She had never had a name for where she had died. Only a stark memory of a hospice, underground. Sterile corridors and screams. The stench of blood and viscera. "I don't remember how I got there."

That was not entirely a lie. Lien did remember how she got out. Small and frail and shivering as she was, flesh already warping from the Change. Stumbling out into the chaos of the street. UnChanged were fighting the Changed. Running down alleys, never looking back until she was away, out of the City, out of the territory that would become known as the Scab. The texture of the skin on her legs had turned scaly by the time Lien had walked a day out of ground zero, her hands warped into claws. Lien remembered those years of her life more kindly now than she did then. When she was young, she still walked on two legs.

"But you do remember the general vicinity of it, don't you?"

She didn't. "What makes you think that I want to return?"

"Haven't you wondered about it?" Servertu asked, in his gentle, reasonable voice. "Wondered why you woke up in that room, Changing. Wondered why you remember little of what came before."

"How do you—"

"I've met others like you. Survivors of the Room."

"Suppose I did wonder," Lien conceded warily. "You should have told me this up front."

"Would you have agreed to leave Basa'at?"

Probably not. "Maybe. I could still head back now."

"You're already five thousand taels richer," Servertu reminded her, "and from what I've heard, Dar Lien makes good on her deals."

"The deal was to take you both to the City. Nothing about finding anything within it."

"You'll need us on the return trip," Yusuf said.

"I've gotten out myself before. Isn't that why the two of you even looked for me in the first place?"

"You can't risk a second trip so close to hot Change. Not without our tech," Yusuf said.

"Though I suppose we do need you more," Servertu said.

Yusuf sighed. "You are *so* bad at negotiation."

"I don't like pretences," Servertu said, apologetic.

Despite herself, Lien had to grin. There was something otherworldly about Servertu, with his naive airs and his neat little voice. The man sounded as though he belonged in one of those Last Summer inforiums, or as a Minister somewhere out East with a small and gentle flock of Godfearers.

"Sun's out. Get me kitted," Yusuf said.

The saddle and gear went back over Yusuf, the black case last. Yusuf was a bounty hunter-turned guardian, perhaps. Lien had seen the sort now and then, tagging along on supply runs for the bloodsport. It hardly ever ended well, and Raahi had no patience for them. Servertu curled a gloved hand on one of Yusuf's spines. Instead of hauling himself up, he touched Yusuf's elbow. Yusuf bent his head, ear pressed to Servertu's lips, listening. He straightened up and waited for Servertu to mount up, then started briskly towards the ramp.

The clouds above them were thicker closer to the Scab, throwing muddy shadows over the canals. Lien missed the sun, even though Crows wouldn't fly out even during a grey morning. One less thing to worry about. Ugly as the morning was, their proximity to the Scab raised Servertu's spirits. He drew his hood back from over his head, asking after sup run stories. Lien obliged to pass the time. Yusuf said nothing at all through her recounting of the last run. An almost clean job, in and out with only one casualty. Psychon trap.

"Raahi doesn't hail from Basa'at?" Servertu asked.

"He makes what money he can from the sup run and spends the rest of the time living it up in Kandan, I think. I never asked. As long as he swung by Basa'at on his way to the Scab and picked me up for the job," Lien said.

"Haven't you ever thought about going Eastwards?" Servertu asked, sounding genuinely curious. "If you worked as a scout in, say, Subterra, you could earn a great deal from the Militia."

"I'm used to the Scab," Lien declared. It was another lie. She was far too Changed to work Eastwards, and she knew it. Surely Servertu knew it.

"What did you haul the last time?" Yusuf asked.

"We got lucky. Military cache. Small one out of the Last Summer. Fair find. Raahi's mostly decent with the split. I took my share in taels." She'd used that money to expand her provision shop. "Better than the last run. Mostly datapacks. Yusuf probably even saw some of them in my shop."

"Surely—" Servertu began. Yusuf held up a hand, coming to an abrupt halt that jarred his passenger against one of the spines.

Lien squinted through the grey light to the barren road ahead of them. There. In the distance. An untidy heap on the ground.

Digging her eyeglass out of her pack, Lien focused until she could make out the dark smear. It was close to the entrance of the Vault. Rotting, oily feathers were torn and strewn on the ground. Its spindly and misshapen wings were broken in vast swathes of black and brown over the dirt. Its brains had been dashed out over the soil in muddy grey clumps, and its serrated beak still hung open. Great rents had been torn into its flanks, still oozing black blood. Vestigial wings and limbs had been ripped off and torn, and its scorpion-like tail was crushed into the concrete. A dead Crow.

"Got into a fight with another Crow. Was chased out here. Died from sun exposure," Lien guessed.

Servertu reached out, and Lien wordlessly passed him the glass. He studied the tableau with open curiosity. "Surely it died from the mortal wound to its head."

"That? That won't even slow one of them. Those birds. You could chop off a wing and a foot and they'd keep going. They're more like yaoguai than any living thing. But they hate each other as much as any sane person would hate them, thank the Changer," Lien said.

"It's dead?" Servertu asked doubtfully.

"Sun's out. It's dead."

Passing the monstrous hulk in death was still a tense affair. The Crow would have stood a hand taller than Yusuf in life. Besides, psychons liked to collect the oily feathers of dead Crows as trophies. The sour rot-stink of the giant corpse lingered lazily over their shoulders as they made their way into the musty gloom of the Vault, its subterranean maw barely wide and high enough for Yusuf to pass. Light filtered through the occasional grating or collapsed ceiling. Lien found the Vault a comforting place. A boundary zone, where it wasn't still too late for her to retreat.

"Tight squeeze. Messy if there's trouble," Yusuf said.

"Psychons don't venture below ground. Crows like to roost in the abandoned towers of the City, high up, wherever there's shelter from the sun. For everything else, this is too far East. This is as safe as the Scab can get. That's why we use it," Lien said.

"Safe?" Yusuf asked.

"Some ghulkins and mutates in here, sure. They're not often aggressive." Not towards a full sup run, anyway. "Outside the Vault's another story though. Bigger packs."

"Raahi used this entrance for years?" Servertu asked. Lien nodded. "Haven't the local… residents found out about it too?"

"Nope. We cleared a tunnel through it ourselves, the first time. That was messy. Never been bothered since, as long as we go through it during the day."

Servertu nodded earnestly, which was, of course, the moment when life decided to directly contradict Lien. A low and sibilant hiss echoed down the dim corridors towards them. Yusuf tensed up.

"Ghulkin," Lien said, resigned.

Yusuf opened the slim case and drew out an ugly rifle. Sleek, slim design, evil-looking and charcoal dark. Made to be simple to strip down and clean, though they often jammed more often than pre-Summer gear. Those were hard to come by now.

"Does that work?" Lien asked.

Yusuf snorted. "No. Brought a useless gun into Changelands. Of *course* it works."

"Good for us," Lien shot back, "except if you fire that in here, you'd bring down every ghulkin on us for miles. Psychons, too."

"Last resort. Let's move."

CHAPTER THREE

The ghulkin numbered three, hunkered over the corpse of a Crow. They hissed and snapped at each other as they fed. The ghulkin crouched in a dried sewage canal, oblivious to the old filth around them. Their hairless orange skin pulled tight over their distended limbs, their eyeless heads more jaw than skull. Sunlight filtered down through a jagged groove in the ceiling, drawing a patchy pool of light on a narrow walkway over an adjacent canal. Yusuf studied the ghulkin, then the pathway. He lowered the muzzle of his rifle towards the ground, gesturing curtly with his free hand towards the adjacent canal. Lien relaxed with a nod. So they weren't opting to engage.

Servertu watched the feeding creatures with something like pity on his soft face. The ghulkin ignored their presence and the loud clops of Yusuf's hooves as they picked their way down the adjacent canal and out of sight. Lien scuttled to the front to take the lead. The Vault's sturdy construction tended to withstand Change, and she remembered the dank corridors intimately. The main drainage tunnels that were wide and high enough for Yusuf to pass were few. Some were a tight squeeze overhead, Yusuf having to splay out his hooves awkwardly and duck his head, cursing softly under his breath. Once, Servertu tried to dismount, murmuring something about weight. Yusuf's palm darted back to still him, pressing high up over Servertu's knee with something akin to possessiveness.

When they stopped for a midday break in an old maintenance room, Yusuf tugged down his scarf to eat instead of turning away from them both. An old, badly healed scar tipped up half of his mouth into a permanent half-smirk.

"You could've gotten that fixed wherever you did your prefab job," Lien said, motioning towards her mouth.

Yusuf stamped one of his hind legs, ignoring her. Servertu steadied himself and dismounted, walking over on unsteady feet to sit on an old crate. He waved away Yusuf's look of disapproval and said, "Yusuf's no longer welcome at Yaran."

"Servertu," Yusuf muttered.

"He's a Paladin, isn't he?"

"No," Servertu said, chewing on his energy bar. He smiled wryly as Lien opened her mouth to ask another question. "Discretion, Miss Lien."

"Just trying to find out how good Yusuf will be in a tight corner."

"Better than you," Yusuf growled. He subsided when Servertu raised a palm.

"He's very capable." Servertu finished his energy bar in precise bites and pulled a small red book out from under his cloak. It had a yellow pencil strapped to its spine. He flipped the book open nearly to the middle and started to write industriously, oblivious to Lien's astonishment.

Books she had seen, during sup runs. Raahi tended to ignore them or, if he had to, gather them as a ready source of fuel. She had never seen anyone write in one of them. Or write at all. Servertu's handwriting was as neat as he was, all angular letters in crabbed lines. He looked up as he sensed her interest, smiling self-consciously.

"A memory aid. I would've liked to study the ghulkin longer if we could."

Yusuf grunted. "Only good for studying if they're dead. Even then, only with a flamethrower."

"Thought the two of you have seen ghulkin before," Lien said.

"I've never seen ghulkin eat a Crow," Servertu said.

"They'll eat anything that's dead. Or almost dead." Lien pointed out.

"Yes, but how often have you seen a dead Crow? And now two within the day. Fascinating. Selangor was indeed the turning point."

"Bloody disaster. Ghulkin overran the Fastness," Yusuf said, for Lien's benefit. "Messy."

"The Fastness? It's been there since before the Last Summer, hasn't it? I thought it was impregnable," Lien said, startled.

Yusuf shook his head. "It's gone."

"There was a stormflux. Swept the outer courtyard of the Fastness. Caused the Change to run hot enough in the outer perimeter to Change the Fastness' defender into ghulkin. Worse, in cases," Servertu said. He looked grim.

Lien shuddered. A stormflux was bad news for any resident of the Scablands and their like. As ground-level clouds of charged mist that carried the Change, they warped whatever they touched. "I haven't seen a stormflux for eight years. The last one passed under Basa'at, easy. Wasn't the Fastness also built on high?"

"It was. The Quarantined Cities like to think that they understand the Change and the Changelands. We actually don't understand them at all."

Servertu wasn't from Jinsha'an. Didn't sound like it. Tema'ase Citadel, maybe. Or Kandan. One of the Quarantined Cities. Where fifteen thousand taels were little more than loose change to the wealthy, easy money to barter for a Changing scout's services.

"Do we need to? Understand them?"

Servertu looked surprised that she had asked. "Of course. Preferably before the Changelands start to expand."

"Expand…!" Panic ticked briefly through Lien before reason set in. "That won't happen. I've lived outside the Scab all my life. Boundaries haven't budged."

"For now," Servertu tucked his pencil and book away. "The ghulkin being here, the dying Crows, they're all symptoms. Another era of Great Change is coming. Selangor might just be a precursor."

"Shouldn't the Citadel be warned? Or Kandan? Everyone?"

"If we can find the evidence. Life in the Citadel—or in Kandan—is quite different from life out in the Scablands. Their citizens would prefer to pretend that the rest of you out in the wastes don't exist. Prefab and junction tech has improved in leaps and bounds over the last few years. If you have the taels, Change is merely an annoyance to be fixed as easily as you can breathe."

Lien tried to imagine that. An entire city of people who looked like Servertu—UnChanged. Who could fix any mutation in their bodies the way they might fix their hair in the morning. Who never needed to worry about the Change's final curse, when it touched the brain and turned its host into a mindless monster to be exiled out into the Changelands.

"I can't believe that," Lien said.

Servertu nodded. "It's hard for anyone Outside to believe. But a Great Change would affect everyone. Privileged or not."

"No one even knows what caused the first Great Change."

"There are theories," Servertu said. He smiled without looking over his shoulder when Yusuf sniffed. "Time will prove one of them right."

"Should have stayed in the Archives with your books," Yusuf muttered, not without a touch of heat.

"You wouldn't have known what to look out for," Servertu countered. This was another old argument, Lien sensed. One that had festered around the edges.

It was the dry season, and the plants that called the Scab home had withered in the late afternoon sun. They emerged quietly from the western exit of the Vault. Other than the ghulkin, they hadn't run into any incidents. Lien stretched in the sun, glancing at the dark mouth of the tunnel behind her with regret. Beyond this point, there was no easy return. The exit opened up to a shallow, concrete-lined canal. Its walls were long overgrown by thorn and shrub, a thick, sturdy blanket that ran along the canal, as tall on either side as Yusuf.

"Remarkable. I read about this. Saw pictures of the monsoon season. It's still more dramatic than I thought," Servertu said. He stood up in the saddle, a palm balanced against Yusuf's shoulder as he craned his neck this way and that. Yusuf had automatically braced for it without comment, and he stared down Lien when she gawked.

"We wouldn't go this way in the monsoon season. Thorns give off sap when it's that wet out. Turns your mind if you get it on bare skin. Knew a man who tried to eat his own arm just from a drop of it. Chewed off and swallowed a couple of fingers before we could sedate him," Lien said. That had been a fun run. Raahi's crew now ran with huge steel pruning scissors in a supply cart that could be operated from a safe distance, and they never did a run during the monsoons.

"Nothing so hallucinogenic used to exist in this part of the world before the Last Summer. They're safe like this? In the dry season?" Servertu asked, wary.

"Nothing in the Scab is safe." Lien started to walk through the piles of rubble and trash that lined the bottom of the canal. She could see the first rest stop from here, a squat bunker of a warehouse that would have a combi-locked door. Looked intact from here, not looted, burned, or warped. Good sign, though you never knew. Sometimes the psychons got creative. Or the Change could've fused steel into brick.

"How are we going to get through the thorns?" Servertu shaded his eyes. "It looks like it stretches as far as the canal."

"There's a way up due north. We salt the ground each time we come. Should still be open."

"Should?"

"Things in the Scab have a tendency to warp. If there's no way through, we'll have to exit the canal due north and circle around,. It'll be dark before we get to where we want to."

"… This seems to be a rather uncertain way of navigating," Servertu said doubtfully.

"Normally it won't matter. A full team of spotters, muscle and scouts can survive for a bit out in the dark, especially this far out of the City. But it should be fine. It's still the dry season," Lien said.

They passed another Crow body, an hour into the walk. This one had been dead for longer. It was picked to its bones, warped cages of white calcium stretched long and hollow. To Lien's annoyance, Servertu insisted on stopping to make a quick sketch in his book. Yusuf planted his hooves firmly on the concrete ground and went still.

"We're exposed out here." Lien looked around warily.

Yusuf shrugged, armour and leather straps creaking as his

shoulders rolled. "Hidden behind the thorn."

"Until we have to breach it for the safehouse, and I'd prefer to do that while there's still enough light to see by."

"Won't take long," Yusuf said. He darted a couple of glances up at the grey sky, his hands tightening briefly on his rifle.

"What's so interesting about that dead monster, anyway?"

"It's possible that large mutates like Crows are a final developmental stage of smaller mutates like ghulkin," Servertu said as he sketched. "That the Change accelerates where the ghulkin gather on the Changelands. Ghulkin, I believe, is the larval stage, from which the rest of the Changeland creatures derive."

Lien pulled a face. "The ghulkin becoming one of these? Don't think so. Ghulkin are about our size. That huge thing is bigger than all of us combined."

"The laws of physics and biology matter little in the Changelands, especially where the Change grows hot. Nowhere else but in the Changelands can the Crows fly. The usual laws of gravity wouldn't allow it," Servertu said earnestly.

Lien glanced at Yusuf, who ignored them both. "The Change takes all people differently. No one's the same. But once the Change reaches the brain… we become ghulkin?" Lien asked. As far as she or anyone else she had known had thought, people who were far too Changed simply just left for the Changelands, where they were presumably killed and eaten by raiders or mutates. Changer knew it was easy enough to die out here when you were lucid. "The ghulkin all look similar."

"I've a theory about that as well." Servertu pointed at the ribcage. "Look at the bone structure of that Crow. See the striations on the—"

There was a distant rustling sound, beyond the thorn. They all tensed, waiting until it passed. Once the world was quiet, Yusuf said, "Enough. Time to go."

"I still want a closer look. You said that we were safe in here," Servertu said.

"Didn't say safe. Said hidden." Servertu sucked in an irritated breath, and Yusuf said, "Servertu, *please*." There was a wiry tension to the plea, the faintest edge of fear.

"… fine," Servertu said. He closed his book. "You're overreacting."

Yusuf started to walk before Servertu even tucked the book away. He said nothing, his hands clenched tightly over his rifle. Servertu set his jaw. He pushed his book back under his cloak and shot Lien an apologetic look, as if embarrassed on Yusuf's behalf. Lien returned a blank-eyed stare in response. She wanted no part in their quarrels.

The rest of the day's walk to the salted path took place in silence. Lien breathed out in a rush when she saw the gap, picking up her pace—then came to a sharp halt as she saw a faint flicker of movement within the thicket of thorns. The sudden stop saved her. A gob of orange acid splashed where she would have been, hissing and bubbling over the concrete. Lien let out a yelp of shock, leaping back and drawing her daggers.

A small pack of ghulkin burst out from the path. Their backs were burned and blistered black. The ghulkin shrilled and hissed as they charged, long limbs swinging their lithe bodies forward in leaping hops. Yusuf roared in response, bounding forward. Servertu hunched down, holding on to Yusuf's saddle. His knees were pressed to Yusuf's flanks, and he made no sound as Yusuf charged the rest of the ghulkin pack. Yusuf smashed the lead ghulkin into the concrete with flailing hooves. Whirling with deft grace, Yusuf swung the heavy stock of his rifle into the next, dashing out its brains. He spun around, slapping a third out of the air with a powerful kick from his hindquarters that knocked it squealing into the thorns. Another swing of the rifle took care of the fourth. The last, hidden in the thicket, scrambled back. It wriggled into the thorny undergrowth, yelping with fear.

Yusuf came to a halt, grimacing at the orange gore staining the stock of his rifle. He wiped it down with a rag that Servertu passed him from the saddlebags. The used cloth was tossed aside, then Yusuf turned to regard Lien. The scarf around his neck had dropped low, and his uneven smirk was frightening under the shadow of his hat.

"Exercise," Yusuf said, as though he hadn't just destroyed a ghulkin pack singlehandedly.

"Changer's hairy *asshole*. What are you?" Lien gasped.

Yusuf trotted over to the still writhing ghulkin, dashing in its skull with a well-placed hoof. "Scout goes point," Yusuf said. He tugged the scarf back up over his mouth, calm and still again. He wasn't even breathing hard.

Lien had to concentrate not to flinch as she passed by, pulling herself up onto the salted path through the thorns. The thicket was starting to reclaim the soil, despite the damage. It was still wide enough for Yusuf to pass through, the sound of his hooves dampened on the dusty ground. Waste and rubbish had blown in since the last time Lien had been here. She stepped over old rotting boxes, twisted metal cans, plastic bags, grimy glass bottles.

Behind her, Yusuf was making no real effort to be quiet. Thankfully, they had hours yet to dusk, and the psychons didn't like the thorns. "Ghulkin in the sunlight," Yusuf was saying quietly to Servertu. "Here."

"They were still burned. But only blackened. They were adapting."

"Wouldn't call that adapting."

"It might explain the dead Crows. And the Edoras in the Bakgut Plains. The yoles in Subterra. They're being pushed to evolve. Even in ways that they're not currently suited. The next Great Change is imminent," Servertu said.

"That doesn't matter right now, does it? As long as the Changelands don't expand. Mutation's always run rife in the Scab anyway," Lien said.

"It depends on what the next Great Change's purpose is. Or if it even has a purpose." Servertu's face lit up as he spoke. "It's been a topic of continuous contention back in the Archives. Whether chaos itself can be said, paradoxically, to have a purpose. Some sort of ultimate end. Ironically."

"And what do you think?" Lien asked.

"Don't get him started. He'll talk your ear off for a week," Yusuf said.

"I'm close to a definitive conclusion," Servertu said, injured.

"So things like the... ghulkin in the sun. They've been happening everywhere? In the Changelands? This is the first I've heard of it."

"I'm not surprised. Travel between the Changelands isn't so

common. Especially not to Basa'at. We heard about it, but we haven't seen proof of it until now," Servertu said.

"So you think you can find the reason behind all that in the City?" Lien asked sceptically.

Servertu nodded. "Part of the reason. The last piece of the puzzle. I hope."

CHAPTER FOUR

"Something's not right. Someone's been here. Those tracks look recent," Lien said.

Yusuf raised his rifle, scanning the area. The safehouse was a high-ceilinged warehouse, once used to store boxes of disassembled furniture. It was large enough for supply carts to fit inside. Raahi had neatly partitioned the warehouse over time into living quarters and storage sections, with space left over to spare. There was even a small cache of basic rations and ammunition within a combination-locked safe in the foreman's room, suspended on the mezzanine floor. A walkway ran the length of the mezzanine, boarded along the sides for cover. The windows were barred.

"Empty," Yusuf said. He looked at the tracks that had disturbed the dust. "Full sup train?"

"Dozen people at least. Vehicles too. But they didn't pass through Basa'at. I would've known," Lien said. Was it Raahi? He'd come to the Scab without her?

Yusuf twisted to look at Servertu. "Serverun."

"How long ago?" Servertu asked Lien.

"I'm thinking two days. Maybe three," Lien said, inspecting the ashes within a fire pit.

Yusuf scowled, turning around to kick the door closed behind him with more force than it warranted. "Must have been running hot since the Citadel, if they've been bypassing outpost towns."

"Or running low," Servertu said.

"What's going on? Who's Serverun?" Lien asked.

"We're not the only ones headed to the City. Serverun's a...

competitor," Servertu said.

"Changer, why? There's nothing in the City. Unless you're interested in pre-Summer tech. And even that's not generally worth precious much for all this trouble—you might not find anything useful. Most workable stuff, you can get off Raahi—"

"There's more in the City than pre-Summer tech," Servertu interrupted. He dismounted, wincing and stretching, rubbing his lower back with the heels of his palms.

"This Room that you're looking for? Are they after it too?"

Servertu nodded. "We'll have to step up our pace, if possible. We need to beat Serverun to the City."

"Look at this," Yusuf pawed at marks on the ground from what looked like long, parallel treads. "Broken out the big guns. APCs."

"What are those?" Lien asked.

"Armoured Personnel Carriers. Vehicles. Turret on the top." At Lien's blank stare, Yusuf said, "What?"

"There are vehicles out there that still work? What do people do for fuel?"

"Solar. Not many outside Quarantine Cities," Yusuf conceded.

"What's in the Room?" Lien demanded, but Servertu was staring hard at the tracks, frowning to himself. Yusuf trotted off. He circled the warehouse space, checking the entrances and the windows.

"This is one of Raahi's safehouses?" Yusuf asked.

"Yes," Lien said.

"How many people know the combination key?"

Lien rubbed a claw over her forehead. "Raahi, me... a couple of the other scouts, and Fatima. Raahi's lieutenant. Only people who've run with Raahi for ten years, at the least."

"Door wasn't forced." Yusuf jerked his chin at the door. "Any of the other scouts might've been tempted to do another Scab run?"

Lien let out a harsh laugh. "With the money you were offering me? Could be any of them. Could be Raahi himself. And if it was Raahi, we're fucked. No one knows the Scab better than Raahi."

"You don't seem to think that it is."

"Raahi likes to run with people he knows. I'd have heard of it if he was going."

"You always go on runs with him? Into the Scab?" Yusuf asked.

"Most times, yes. The last time I didn't…" Lien gestured at her thorax.

"Safehouse would have a cache, won't it? Check it."

Lien climbed up the narrow steps carefully, jointed feet clicking on the rusted metal. She hauled herself into the mezzanine room. The safe clicked open neatly when she input the code, and she studied the contents for a while before closing the heavy door again, crossing out to the walkway.

Below, Servertu was sitting down on a crate. Yusuf was kneeling, his two front legs tucked under his bulk, hind legs planted carefully. He was massaging Servertu's right thigh, big hands stroking lovingly up above his kneecap. Servertu was writing in his sketchbook, as though oblivious to the way he was being touched, the way Yusuf's head was bent close.

She was intruding. Lien backed quietly into the mezzanine room, waiting until she was bored before finally emerging again. She made sure to bang about as she headed down the walkway. Once she was back on the ground floor, Yusuf was at the fire pit, working on the firestarter. Neither looked at Lien as she approached. After a moment's hesitation, Lien made her way to Yusuf to help with the setup.

"Cache wasn't raided," Lien said. Better than that—it had been restocked with higher-grade supplies. Doubt wormed in. Only Raahi ever bothered to restock the caches. Everyone else was just a contractor, after all. Besides, very few people had the combination.

"Means the sup run was well-prepared," Yusuf said.

"Looks like it."

"Is it Raahi?"

"Don't know. Does it matter?"

Yusuf tilted his head, surprised at the sharpness in her tone. "No."

"Good."

"We have rations to spare. If you'll like. It'll be better than dry rations or the bars," Servertu said. A peace-offering.

"Sure," Lien said. No one turned down free food or water from an ally in the Scablands. "Thanks."

It didn't take long for the firestarter to heat up. Soon the pot of water was boiling merrily. Lien used one of her purif pills out of politeness. Yusuf backed off to make another circuit around the boarded windows.

"Psychon territory?" Yusuf asked as Lien poured the ration powder and cubes into the pot. She'd seen packs like these only on Raahi runs. After a few minutes' stirring in hot water, the powder turned into a satisfying, chunky soup. Her stomach rumbled within her thorax, eager after two days of dry rations.

"Yep."

"Hopefully, the psychons would be more interested in a large, visible contingent. Pity." Servertu sighed.

"Pity?" Lien echoed incredulously.

"I would've liked to see a psychon. Scientifically speaking, it's a phenomenon unique to the Scab. Quite interesting, too, how primitive junction tech served to create an entire subculture."

"I wouldn't call it primitive tech. They stuff themselves in metal suits and shock themselves. They're more dangerous than the ghulkin. At least the ghulkin have Changed brains," Lien said sourly.

"There's that. but from a sociological standpoint, it's rather fascinating. Welded into their metal suits as they are, several bodily functions have become… quite unusual. And of course, the Change doesn't allow them to reproduce, as they're all quite sterile. So they resort to banditry to swell their ranks, but—"

"They're cannibals and murderers. No pain threshold and they don't get frightened. So I've heard," Yusuf said, when Lien stared at him. "Hopefully they go after Serverun. Slow him down."

"I wouldn't wish the psychons on anyone," Lien said, stirring the pot as the soup thickened up. "Grub's up."

They ate in silence. It was better than any ration pack that Lien had tried off Raahi, and she tried to savour it. She would have licked her bowl clean if she could. Yusuf and Servertu both pretended not to notice. When Servertu offered her the last portion, Lien's hunger won the field over politeness.

Yusuf cleaned off the plates with a non-hydrated pocket rinser, a handy bit of Jinsha'an tech. Lien settled near Servertu, peering at his book. He held it up to show her, crabbed notes wrapped around a beautifully accurate drawing of the thorns. Lien smiled softly. Basa'at wasn't exactly a place where art flourished. The only exposure she had to beautiful things like this was if she got lucky on a sup run.

"I saw a picture book once," Lien said. "It was almost intact. Colour pictures, brighter than any colourstat, even after the years. It was about… Changed animals, and an UnChanged boy. Raahi said that the title was Where the Wild Things Are."

"Ah." A brief touch of hunger crossed Servertu's face. "I'm not familiar with that title. Did you take it with you?"

"No. In sup runs, you only take quota." She couldn't read anyway.

"Would you remember where that book is?" Servertu asked eagerly. From the fire, Yusuf cleared his throat pointedly. "That is. If it's on the way."

"It won't be on our way, if it's even still there. Arjun once told me—he's worked muscle for various sup runs, various Changelands—he'd seen a whole building full of books. Over in Selangor, I think it was."

"Very likely." Servertu's face fell. "If it was in Selangor, it's unlikely to still be intact any longer. The wealth of knowledge once known to Man… To what depths have we fallen. Turning in the gyre," Servertu said, wistful. "We're now a falcon without a falconer."

Lien glanced at Yusuf, but Yusuf's gaze was fixed on Servertu's face, his eyes unreadable behind his goggles. "Serverun might try to travel at night," Yusuf said, making no attempt to hide the abrupt change of subject.

"Travelling at night is suicide," Lien said.

"Not with the appropriate gear, it isn't."

"But—"

"Whether he is or not is of little consequence," Servertu interrupted, "since *we* can't travel by night. We'll just have to try to catch up the best we can."

"Or we turn back. Pay Miss Lien for her time. We're at least two days behind them, and we can't hope to catch up by going the long way," Yusuf said.

"Or we could turn back only when there's proof that the situation is hopeless," Servertu countered.

Yusuf grunted. "You saw the tracks."

"We don't know what their situation is. The Scab is treacherous even for the well-equipped, according to Miss Lien. All the Changelands are. I wouldn't discount our luck quite as yet," Servertu said.

"Serverun's that much of a big shot?" Lien asked. She tried to imagine having the 'appropriate gear' to travel at night. What would that even be? Were 'APCs' that powerful?

"He's got the backing of the Citadel. A loud proponent of Recidivism. It's rather unfortunate. He is, after all, an otherwise rather reasonable fellow," Servertu said.

"Oh yes. He did so very reasonably try to get us killed in Selangor," Yusuf muttered. "Asshole."

Servertu shook his head. "That wasn't proven."

"… all right," Lien said, very slowly. "So this Serverun, if it even is him, is going to be trouble."

"Yah," Yusuf said, even as Servertu said, "Still not proven."

"And he's got… a full team, and Citadel tech?"

"On the bright side, that'll probably make him easy to spot. If we ever run into his party," Servertu said.

Would Raahi—or whoever it was—chance moving at night? With sufficient tech? Lien wouldn't have dared to. "If this guy is reckless enough to take an overland route in the night, we'll probably see the evidence of that sooner or later."

The morning made it obvious that they were on someone else's tail. The APCs had cut a wide swathe through one of the erstwhile safe routes, flattening trash, rubble, and thorn alike. Ruins and thorns cut off Lien's line of sight, making it difficult to see further than a couple of blocks at once, but in the distance, she could see circling dark specks. Crows, attracted to something large on the ground.

"Not a good sign," Yusuf said, following her gaze. "Why aren't they attacking?"

"There's a healthy degree of self-preservation in all mutates." Servertu scribbled something into his book.

"Just because they can be scared of something doesn't mean that they're like people," Yusuf said. There was a hard edge to his voice. "Animals know when to be frightened of something."

"Normally, no one messes with the Crows other than other Crows. That's probably what Servertu means," Lien said.

Yusuf's scowl was visible even over his grey scarf. Servertu shot Lien a grateful look and said, "This must have been the industrial sector. Warehouses and the docks beyond, feeding into the Rinse. It must have once been a hub of trade. Imagine that. More people than in the Citadel, all on the move, living in towers like those beyond us, driving over these streets."

"How many people are there in the Citadel?" Lien asked.

Servertu's expression took on a dreamy cast. "Oh… no more than half a million, I think. It's rather sad."

"Half a *million?*" Lien had never seen any more than a few hundred people in one place all at once. That had been on a rare trip decades back, when she had once had the chance to visit Jinsha'an. "You're kidding me."

"No, no. Easily. Kandan as well. The birth rate hasn't been improving though," Servertu said, puzzled by Lien's astonishment. "Places like the Citadel and the City used to contain populations of up to fifteen million, according to the Archives. Before the Last Summer."

Lien couldn't even imagine one million of anything, let alone people. UnChanged people. She struggled silently with the thought, turning it in her mind as she walked, trying to think first of a rank of ten people, then twenty, then a hundred.

"Somebody had fun," Yusuf said, as they climbed over a small hill of rubble onto a concrete overpass. Beyond, black stains were liberally splashed over a forcibly cleared boulevard. Bullet marks and small impact craters peppered the asphalt.

"No bodies?" Servertu asked.

"Out here?" Yusuf gestured at the dark, empty openings to adjacent buildings. Some were covered in thorn, some gaping open to grimy foyers. "Ghulkin probably towed them off." He trotted over to the nearest stain, circling around it. "See that. Bodies were dragged away." Yusuf kicked at a pitted shoulder plate that lay upended on its side, leather straps burned off. "Psychons came out worse."

"Looks like it." Lien studied the swathe of devastation with unease. "Changer. Maybe we should switch routes. Your friend Serverun will have stirred the psychons up something awful. They'll be watching this route."

"What's the delay? If we switch?" Yusuf asked.

"We'll lose at least a couple of days."

Yusuf grunted, sounding satisfied, but Servertu shook his head. "Speed is paramount right now."

"No, your safety is paramount," Yusuf retorted.

"There aren't any psychons in sight. They've probably retreated to lick their wounds," Servertu said.

"Or they might be out in force, looking to take out their frustrations on someone else. 'Sides, if you're not friendly with Serverun, any half-decent sup run will have scouts up front and out back. We'll be seen," Lien said.

Servertu exhaled. "All right then. We'll do it your way, Miss Lien. But if we could pick up the pace any other way… please."

Lien nodded. She led them down an alley that would drop them back towards the canal network. A winding route to the Rinse, one that was hopefully less frequented by psychons. "'Least we know that it's definitely led by someone out of Raahi's team. That safehouse, and then this route. They're taking the fastest leg," Lien said.

"Can we beat them to the City?" Servertu asked.

"Not if we have to circle around them."

"If we go close to the Rinse? That cuts right to the City doesn't it?"

Lien pulled a face. "Theoretically, yes, if we can follow the Rinse, we might be able to reach the City before Serverun."

"Then I think that it's a chance that we have to take. The City is a huge sprawl, and they'd be slowed down closer to it. The roads are thick with old car wrecks, aren't they?" Servertu gestured in Serverun's general direction.

"Yah. They might not be able to drive whatever they're driving into the City. Though I'm not in a hurry to run into whatever it is that can keep a flock of Crows circling up high," Lien said.

"We're not here to confront them. At the very least, Yusuf would be quite cross if that were so." Servertu smiled.

"You've never cared about that," Yusuf retorted.

"This one would beg to differ."

"Why do you say that sometimes?" Lien asked absently, as she teetered her way up a pile of boxes and rubble, searching for safe footing. "Say 'this one'? Is it a Citadel thing? You don't have an accent."

"Ah…" Servertu trailed off. He sounded uncomfortable enough that Lien glanced back over her shoulder at him, but couldn't see further than Yusuf's impassive bulk. "It is an… accur… It is, shall we say, an affectation."

"Least weird thing about him," Yusuf said. The crook of his mouth arched up on the unbroken edge as Servertu let out a badly stifled squawk of indignation. The sound hiccuped into a soft gasp as they emerged from the alley into another boulevard, this one choked with old wrecks.

The corpses of Crows littered the street. Seven of them, smashed into the roofs of the wrecked cars or draped over the buildings beyond. Unlike the psychon bodies, these hadn't been dragged away. Lien twitched in disgust as she crossed the wide street, trying to give the nearest body a large berth.

"The ghulkin took the psychons, but not the Crows?" Servertu leaned over in his saddle for a closer look.

"Maybe they couldn't carry everything and the psychons are better eating." Yusuf glowered at the closest, rotting body with distaste. "Look. Exit wound size. Hole punched through, as big as my hand. High calibre rifle. Anti-materiel. Crows must have gotten too close."

Lien looked up at the distant cloud of Crows. "Why don't they just keep shooting? Ah. I see. That's clever."

"What?" Yusuf asked.

"Psychons hate Crows. If they see them, even roosting ones, they won't come close. I was in a sup run once that scattered a knot of psychons just by luring in a couple of Crows. But a whole flock of them? That takes balls of steel."

"Or a great deal of ignorance," Yusuf said, with a sour look over his shoulder. "Serverun-level of ignorance."

"That's inaccurate," Servertu said.

Yusuf merely shook his head, flicking his tail as he crossed the boulevard. "Stirring up the locals like this is always bad."

"Thought you were hoping Serverun would draw attention to himself," Lien said.

Yusuf nodded. "Hoped he drew the psychons. Not every godsdamned giant mutate in the vicinity. That's just bad news for everyone."

CHAPTER FIVE

The psychons were definitely following Serverun's contingent, even if the Crows were keeping them from closing in. Lien saw not a hair of the metal-clad zealots as they circled around the main industrial thoroughfare towards the Docklands, one of the lesser mouths of the Rinse. They did still skirt around watchtowers and outposts, just to be safe.

The second rickety watchtower was reinforced haphazardly with corrugated metal and adorned with necklaces of bleached, misshapen bone. "These should be manned. Look at the generators. They were maintained up until recently," Lien said.

Servertu began sketching the watchtower furiously into his book. "Isn't this interesting? Humanity descends into tribal practices by default, a sort of primitive general code. But by all reports, the psychons aren't gender-differentiated."

"The only thing psychons respect is strength. And they're tribal, certainly, but they're not one tribe, but many. This is Skinhawks territory. We passed into it half an hour back. They don't watch the backdoor too hard, but we should've seen something of them by now." Lien couldn't hide her unease.

"A trap?" Yusuf asked.

Lien shook her head. "Not how they work. I don't like it. Is it another one of those symptoms you talk about? Are they all dead or something?" No bodies though. Had the ghulkin dragged everything off somewhere?

"Possibly. To date, I've mostly seen symptoms in the form of unusual stormflux and increased mutagenic results in existing mutates. I haven't quite had the chance to study its effect on the people actually living inside the Changelands," Servertu said.

"Probably not a good idea." Yusuf frowned.

"If they're all gone," Servertu said reasonably, "then it'll be safe to do so, won't it? We should at least investigate one of their domiciles. Learn what happened. Whether they left, and perhaps why."

"Rather not." Lien shuddered. "We don't have an APC. Besides, didn't you say that time was the essence?"

"… true." Servertu deflated visibly. "Pity. It'll be a mistake to guess without data."

They left the Junkyard and crossed through a broken wire fence into the Docklands proper, stopping to rest in an old shipping container. Just before the Rinse was a gigantic ship at the dry docks, forever immobile. It towered over the stacks of colourful containers, all fading under the grey sun. More wrecks lined the Rinse, as dead as the vehicles that choked the empty streets. Lien knew them all by heart, even though she couldn't see them through the maze of abandoned containers. This wasn't the usual route up to the City for a Raahi run, but once they'd taken this way there and back during a time when the psychon presence around the Vault had run too hot. The air smelled of sun-warmed rust and the cloying, coppery-rot stink of the distant Rinse.

"Hard to believe those things used to be everywhere on the oceans. Those huge ships," Yusuf said.

"Humanity's fallen quite far past its golden age." Servertu's energy bar was left unfinished by his side as he sketched the ship.

"Eat," Yusuf chided. Servertu did so reluctantly, though only after Yusuf nudged his knee.

"You ever heard of Rinse-sight?" Lien asked.

"Heard you start to see things that aren't there. When you get close to the big river through the Scab." Yusuf gestured in the general direction of the Rinse.

Lien nodded, grim. "It's why I was hoping to avoid cleaving to the Rinse for as long as we could. Rinse-sight often draws you dangerously close to the Rinse. Changer, I hope whatever you've got that'll protect us up close is going to work."

"It will. I'm looking forward to viewing Rinse-sight. It's

possibly not quite hallucinogenic. A normal hallucination is private, while everyone sees the same Rinse-vision. A popular academic theory is that the Change runs so hot in the Rinse that there's a time distortion." Servertu scribbled a note. "It's not unique to the Scab. Any moving body of water deep in the Changelands generates its version of Rinse-sight."

"Whatever it is, there's a reason why we usually stay away from that thing. Even discounting hot Change. The psychons and the mutates have the sense to stay away from the Rinse too. Hopefully, the Docks will be the last bit of real estate where we actually might run into anything."

"This place is usually patrolled?" Yusuf asked. He scanned the wire link fence. It divided asphalt and dirt, and at its foot on either side was a small hill of worn cardboard, plastic and metal cans. Debris from another time, now sun-blasted into tangled heaps.

Lien grimaced. "It's not normally this quiet. Doubt they'd *all* have chased after the APCs. They keep to their territories."

"So something happened." Yusuf shifted his weight on his hooves uneasily.

"We should keep moving."

They skirted yet another empty sentry point before Yusuf's own curiosity finally got the better of him. He circled back to the watchtower, ducking from cover to cover. Lien watched their backs, checking their blind spots until they finally came to the welded ladder up to the sentry point. The lookout sat on top of two rows of stacked shipping containers. Barely visible from the lip of the topmost container was a pile of sandbags, stacked around an empty chair and large worn umbrella shade.

Servertu made as if to dismount, but Yusuf reached back sharply to grab his knee. He looked at Lien, who nodded reluctantly. They *did* need to know what had happened to the psychons. Find out whether whatever had caused their disappearance was still here. Lien made the climb as silently as she could, Yusuf covering her with his rifle, hauling herself up to the second row. The metal was hot under the tips of her legs. Lien braced for an attack as she glanced cautiously into the open shipping container beneath the sentry chair, then breathed out.

Clear.

"Looks empty," Lien called down. "I'm going to check it for supplies."

Yusuf nodded at her. Lien scuttled into the container, daggers at the ready. The sentry outhouse-container had housed at least two people, psychons both, judging from the psychons' total disinterest in personal sanitation. The container stank of semi-human waste, sweat and worse. The stink was so chokingly thick that Lien hastily undid the sash at her hair and wrapped it around her mouth and nose. The psychons had slept on filthy cots that lined the floor to Lien's right, covered here and there with piles of stinking scavenged blankets. To the left with a haunch of rotting meat sat on a desk. Few weeks old, Lien guessed, going by the humming cloud of hungry flies and the smell of maggot rot.

Lien backed out and almost knocked over a small cardboard box of ammunition that sat by the open door. It held a selection of 9mm magazines and assorted boxes of shotgun shells and more. Good scavenge. She stashed as much into her pack as she could carry and peered out.

Yusuf and Servertu were nowhere to be seen.

Lien nearly called out for them. Experience and her own Scabland-grown paranoia stilled her tongue. She backed into the stinking container. Once hidden from view, she peeked out cautiously from the edge. *There.* Perched on the girder of a shipping crane, a row of containers away. A Crow.

There was something wrong about it. Lien squinted against the grey sun, shading her eyes. The Crow was hunched over, weirdly small and misshapen, and wearing armour. A patchy steel breastplate had been strapped over its ribs, a shoulder plate digging over its right wing. Scraps of boiled leather from the ruin of an old vest draped down towards its distended belly. It even had a checkered scarf knotted around a hairless neck. Its beak clacked open and closed in a brittle rhythm.

Who would have put armour on a…?

The Crow turned its flank towards her, and Lien understood. Strapped across its back was the remains of a box Tesla, a small generator-and-coils machine that would juice up a psychon with an electric shock every so often to freeze the Change within them. The remains of other straps had been pecked away, hanging loosely over its tail.

The Crow had been a psychon? Recently? How?

The monster wailed like a human child. It cocked its head, listening and swaying to the echo. It wailed again and again, its wings flaring to their full span in the grey sun. The last cry faded into a hoarse cough as it launched itself heavily into the air.

Lien ducked further back into the container, her heart in her mouth. She offered a hasty prayer to the Changer that was just as quickly ignored. With a heavy thump and a scrabbling of claws, the monster landed above her on the ceiling of the container. There was a sudden clang, a distant crash. It had knocked the sentry's chair over and off the side.

Changer's *balls*.

Lien flattened herself in a corner. She tried not to breathe too often, or too loudly. Maybe the Crow would go away. Maybe—

Another softer cry, one that broke into a breathy giggle. A heavy flap of the wings, a rustle of feathers. A second impact, this time far closer. Just outside the sentry's roost. Lien briefly closed her eyes, gripping her dagger hilts tightly. Even this smaller Crow was too large to fit through the door into the container, but it could certainly fit its hairless neck through. The deadly beak on its bullet-shaped head was as long as Lien's arm.

Lien waited. She had no idea how long she waited, calming herself down. Slowing her breathing, listening to the monster sobbing and singing to itself. Lien looked again around the container for something she could use.

Next to the pile of rags. A gleam of metal, possibly the barrel of a revolver. Lien edged slowly towards it, as quietly as she could. At her second step, the ammunition she had packed into her bag clinked together as her weight shifted.

Rookie mistake.

She'd been too greedy.

Outside, the warble cut off into a harsh, sibilant gasp. The Crow jammed its head and neck through the door, beak parted as it shrilled. Lien scrambled out of its reach with a yelp of fear, swiping the gun as she did so and thumbing the safety—a pistol, not a revolver—but it was jammed tight. She dropped it, whirling and darting away from a stab of its huge beak.

With a cry of desperation, Lien gashed open the Crow's neck with a swipe of her dagger. As it shrieked in fury and outrage, twisting to try and get a better angle, she buried the second dagger up to the hilt in the Crow's right eye with a snarl of her own. It reared back with a sibilant gasp that sounded more surprised than pained. Lien backed off, one dagger left. She knew that a head wound, even one like this, would only just slow a Crow down. She'd have to sever its head, somehow, or—

There was a burst of gunfire. The Crow shuddered and shrieked. Its body heaved and flopped as it froze briefly in indecision, caught between one annoyance and the other. Another burst of gunfire. The Crow backed out, hissing and snarling as it leapt heavily off the container. Yusuf—if it was Yusuf—didn't exactly have the firepower to deal with a Crow. Lien rushed out, scrambling to the edge to look down. Below, Yusuf danced away from the Crow, keeping in its blind spot, harrying it with the occasional burst of fire as Servertu worked feverishly on something that Lien couldn't see. It was a lethal dance. Yusuf just had to be a few seconds too slow and it would be over. Lien had once seen an enraged Crow's beak shear through corrugated metal.

Lien had to try and attract attention back to herself. As she looked helplessly around the container again, Servertu finished whatever he was doing and handed over a small black package to Yusuf. It was tossed at the Crow. The package stuck to its shoulder, high above a wing. Yusuf spun around, sprinting away at a full gallop. He swerved around a row of containers even as the Crow whirled, puzzled and disoriented.

It blew apart.

Lien stared as gobbets of foul meat, parts of a wing, and the Crow's skull splattered across concrete and metal. She ducked back into the stinking container to retrieve the gun. As Lien tried to climb back down, her hands shook against the rungs.

Yusuf trotted up to meet her once she was out of the blast radius. "All right?"

"Ammo," Lien gulped. She clapped a hand over her mouth.

"'Scuse me." Lien hurried away, making it only a few steps before she had to bend against the side of a container and throw up noisily on the ground. Servertu made a sympathetic noise, but thankfully, neither of them said anything. Lien wiped down her mouth with a rag that she tossed aside and walked back over.

"All right?" Yusuf asked again, more gently.

"I might have some ammunition for your rifle." Lien showed them the box of ammo that she had stashed in her pack, as well as the jammed pistol.

"I can try to fix that for you." Servertu adjusted his wire-framed lenses. He took the pistol from her. Yusuf sorted through the ammo and took the .9mms, handing back the rest.

"Thanks for the ammo. And. Sorry," Yusuf said flatly, to Lien's surprise. "Thought it might go away if we lay low for a while. Crows aren't much for patience in the daytime. We didn't mean to make it look like we ran out on you, if that's what you thought."

"I knew you didn't," Lien lied. Yusuf nodded at her. He waited until Lien began to walk before trotting to keep up. "What was the thing that Servertu made? That made the Crow die? That was a handy trick," Lien said.

"Sticky bomb. Very jury-rigged, I'm afraid. I'm glad it worked. We've had that bar of plastic for some time, through some rather deplorable circumstances. I wasn't too sure if it might have degenerated. That was lucky."

"Servertu," Yusuf said, with a faint note of reproach. Lien blanched, aware all over again of her narrow escape, another wave of nausea and dizziness sweeping her. This time she managed to keep her gorge down, breathing deeply and hard through her mouth.

Servertu ducked his head. "Sorry."

"No. Thanks. For the save."

"Was my fault. Wanted to see what was wrong. Just in case we had something up ahead that we had to avoid," Yusuf said.

"I would have made the same call myself. Psychons turning into Crows? Never heard of that. I thought the electricity stopped them from mutating." Was Servertu's so-called Great Change affecting even psychons with Teslas?

"Something smashed up his tesla pack," Yusuf told her.

"I thought maybe that was after he, uh, Changed."

"From what I saw, it looked like sabotage. The wiring was cleanly snipped and the casing was shattered. Turf war, perhaps? Between tribes?" Servertu asked.

"Doubt that. But I don't know. We know damned little about the psychons, other than how to avoid them. That sentry post was only abandoned a few days ago, I think. There was still meat in the container up top," Lien said.

"Assuming that Crow was the sentry." Yusuf glanced uneasily behind them. They kept to the shadows this time, trying to stay away from the wider channels between the rows of shipping containers.

"If ghulkin are from Changed folk... they're usually naked," Lien said.

Servertu nodded. "Biological imperative. They're scavengers and pack hunters. Clothing would slow them down. Especially a psychon's gear. Maybe the Change is starting to bypass the larval stage. If so, it's an incredible step forward."

"As long as it doesn't bypass whatever with us." Lien rubbed her clawed hands over her arms. Nausea still sat sourly in her gut. "Changer, maybe going via the Rinse isn't a great idea after all. Even with whatever the two of you have."

"This sentry post wasn't near enough the Rinse to be affected so greatly, if circumstances were the same as before," Servertu said. He tried to smile at her. "I'm confident."

Lien wasn't comforted. "Well, I'm not. And if psychon territory has turned into Crow territory, we are up shit creek without a paddle."

Servertu winced at Lien's colourful assessment of the situation. Yusuf looked behind them, then up at the sky. "Your lead," he said.

"We'll keep moving," Lien said.

CHAPTER SIX

Lien had first seen the Rinse up close over two decades ago, when she was already a veteran of Scab runs. It had been her first run with Raahi, who had come with impeccable Changelands credentials. His first run into the Scab. The run had gone awry almost immediately once they were out of the Vault—they got caught between an unexpected skirmish between psychons and a huge pack of ghulkin. Sheltering near the Rinse had been a desperate move, one that had cost her the ability to stand with a fully straightened spine, mutating her from the waist down, splitting her legs from two to four. It had warped Raahi's knees and ears.

Raahi had learned his lesson, but Lien had taken longer to learn hers.. Her first and only run without Raahi had ended with Lien out of options and alone, with no way out that she could think of but along the Rinse. As her pelvis turned swollen and bulbous, and her legs split further into segmented limbs, Lien swore that she would never lead a sup run close to the Rinse again. That she would make each run slowly, feeling her way forward. Her mistakes continued to cost her. Her Rinse-changed parts had worsened more rapidly with time, becoming more and more insectile.

Now Lien was breaking every rule about the Scab that she'd ever had to learn. She stood on the ridge of bone-bleached abandoned trucks and cars, overlooking the outer demarcation of the Docklands. A faint frisson of fear shivered up through her twisted spine at the sight of the Rinse.

"Beautiful," Servertu said beside Lien. She nearly fell off

her perch. Absorbed, Lien hadn't heard his approach. Another rookie mistake, and so soon.

"Don't sneak up on people in the Scab," Lien snapped.

Servertu blinked owlishly at her. "Oh. Sorry."

Lien glanced behind them both to the shadow of the truck. Yusuf met her stare, hooves stamping on the asphalt impatiently. Lien lowered her voice. "Your friend's going to wear himself out if you don't get back down."

Servertu gave her a blank look. His eyes turned inexorably back to the Rinse. From this distance, it was a shimmering, oily ribbon, multicoloured and slick. The river's flow was sluggish as it wormed through the Scab. Closer to the Vault, the Rinse kept to its concrete canal. Deeper in where the Change ran hotter, sometimes it meandered up onto 'dry' land, defying the laws of gravity with uncomfortable ease. Beyond the jagged lines of abandoned vehicles and shipping containers, the wide canal of the Rinse made its way eastwards. Out of the Scab and into the Scablands, a band of hot change that sunk itself eventually into the Salt Lake. The banks of the Rinse were clear on the side facing them today, its far side a nightmare of overgrown thorn that had been Changed an uncomfortable fleshy pink. The foliage was so thickened and intricate that it looked like a slow-moving puzzle piece. Another carcass of a ship sat to their right, listing against the banks. It had long shorn its moorings and crushed its dock. Other carcasses sat at further intervals, searching the horizon for the end of entropy.

"Pass that next ridge of cars and the Change will grow really hot." Lien shaded her eyes, trying to breathe evenly through the Rinse-thickened air. Small jabs of panic had started to bubble up in her at uneven intervals. Ever since her close encounter with the Crow-sentry. Lien slipped a hand into her jacket pocket, running her fingers around the edge of the photograph within. She swallowed another bubble of panic.

"Peace." Servertu pressed a hand lightly on her elbow. Lien startled away from him, surprised by the contact. Servertu had made no effort to touch her before.

Below, Yusuf was pointedly not looking at the both of them. Lien hid a faint, sharp smile. "Trouble in paradise?"

"What paradise?" Servertu asked.

"Whatever technological magic device that you've built, you should start it up now, by the way. Just in case. I mean, maybe another arm or leg won't matter so much to me, but you're UnChanged, aren't you?"

"Effectively." Servertu didn't seem in a hurry to move, still studying the Rinse.

Lien looked between the Rinse and her companion-employer, trying to figure out what was so fascinating. There were no psychons or Crows in sight. No life at all. After a while, unnerved, Lien climbed back down. Yusuf glowered at her, clearly blaming her for Servertu's preoccupation.

"Servertu," Yusuf called. Although his voice was flat, the halfer was keyed up. His hooves scattered and shifted constantly on the asphalt.

"Oh, all right," Servertu said, reluctantly climbing down. Yusuf watched anxiously until Servertu was back safe on the asphalt. Servertu rummaged in the saddlebags, drawing out three plain steel bangles. He passed one to Yusuf, another to Lien. Slotted his own up a hand, he pushed it under a sleeve. "There we go."

"You're screwing with me." Lien inspected the bangle. "This is your protection?"

"It works."

"Bullshit," Lien said hotly, flushed with anger and disappointment. "If this is all you've got, we have to turn back. I'll take the rest of my money from you now, thank you very godsdamned much. This is just a piece of jewellery!"

"It isn't. I'll prove it," Servertu told her calmly.

He circled around the truck and started walking briskly towards the Rinse, ignoring Lien's gasp of horror and Yusuf's hiss. The halfer started towards Servertu, but Servertu held up a palm and kept walking. Yusuf tensed up, clenching his fists. Servertu turned and narrowed his eyes. Yusuf backed up a step, prancing nervously.

"Wait!" Lien called after him, but Servertu kept walking. Out towards the margin of where the hot Change would run, as though walking through a park. Lien waited for something horrific to happen. For Servertu's skin to boil, or his hair to start falling off in clumps. For his bones to warp. Nothing happened. Servertu kept walking towards the Rinse itself. Closer and closer. He weaved past the ridge of cars which marked the start of dangerous Change, to the empty contaminated banks. Lien clapped her hands over her mouth to stifle her scream.

"Servertu!" Yusuf broke into stride, eating up the ground. He scooped Servertu up with an arm under his knees. Ignoring Servertu's yelp of indignation, Yusuf wheeled around in a clatter of hooves, thundering back past the ridge of cars. Lien hurried towards them, buoyed by panic and horror.

"Are you both all right? Changer's teeth."

"Servertu," Yusuf said again, harshly. He started to pat Servertu over.

Servertu batted away Yusuf's hands. "I'm perfectly fine, Yusuf." He turned to look at Lien. "Satisfied?"

"I…" Lien put on her bangle. The weight to the air dissipated, making it easier to breathe. "Wait. The air's back to normal.. I'm sorry for doubting you."

"I can see why it might have been hard to believe," Servertu said. He stiffened as Yusuf tugged him closer with an arm around his waist, cheek pressed against the back of Servertu's skull.

"Don't do that again," Yusuf said.

"I was perfectly safe. Selangor was little different, and you were there."

"Don't do that again."

"Yusuf." Servertu patted pointedly at Yusuf's arm. Yusuf reluctantly let up.

"How does it work?" Lien demanded. She touched the tips of her claws to the steel band. "Raahi's been chasing after tech like this for decades. No deal. He searched the Citadel and Kandan."

"It's a proprietary secret," Servertu said. His smile was tired and wry. "Just keep it on and stay close."

"Stay close?" Lien repeated, puzzled. "Is it linked to something else? Something in the saddlebags?"

"Yes." At another nudge from Yusuf, Servertu pulled himself up onto Yusuf's back.

"How close?"

"About twenty metres, give or take. I wouldn't push it if I were you. It's still in its prototype stages."

"I guess it doesn't matter that much. If we can walk safely near the Rinse, we won't be bothered."

"Unless whoever it is with that anti-materiel rifle decides he's had enough fun shooting Crows and starts with us," Yusuf muttered.

"Not unless he climbs up to a vantage point," Lien waved at the abandoned shipping containers around them. "And if he does, he'll be Crow food."

They walked on the perimeter of hot Change. As close as Lien judged would be necessary to be undisturbed by Crow and psychon alike. They moved only as quickly as Lien dared, her scouting constantly ahead for trouble. Servertu chafed at the pace, constantly glancing up at the distant cloud of Crows that indicated Serverun's progress through the Scab. Thankfully, Yusuf sided with Lien. Yusuf had grown jittery since Servertu's demonstration and had been loath to venture far from Servertu's side, even when they found places to rest up for the night.

Days along the Rinse and they were on the outskirts of the Docklands and its industrial zones. The skeletons of abandoned cranes towered behind them, cages of great ribs over the ranks of shipping containers. Lien rather missed the huge metal ridges. The containers had been fair cover. Now that they were past the Docklands, they stood in an overgrown old parkland. Once it had probably been a green buffer that had stood between the industrial zone and everything else. Now it was warped by the Change into thorn and scrub.

Rinse-Sight was at a low ebb. Above the Rinse in the wavering air were hovering faceless outlines. Human-shaped and smoky. Many were still. Some drifted, but none strayed too far. Most stayed in clumps of more than twelve. A few drifted alone, particularly those that were child-sized. Yusuf kept glancing back at the Rinse, thoroughly unnerved. As they stopped for their midday break in the shadow of a rusted silo, he said, "Don't either of you see them?"

Lien glanced over. She had been studying the huge faded red

letters painted over the flank of the silo, which she had seen from much further away when scouting for Raahi. The silo was one of a handful of landmarks that never seemed to warp. This close, it smelled vaguely like drying fish. "See what?"

"Rinse-sight is harmless," Servertu said. He was propped on an old barrel sketchbook on his lap. "It's the other half of the duality. Just a symptom of the schism."

"What schism?" Lien asked.

"A theory of the Change. One of a few. Are you aware of the theory of yin and yang?"

"Light and dark?" Lien traced a circle in the air with a squiggle through it. "I've known people who liked to wear the charms. They thought it was lucky."

"A duality exists within everything and everyone. Light and dark, negative and positive. Some medical theories of the people of the Last Summer and before were rooted in an understanding of the duality. Medicine from duality theory is focused on balancing the duality within someone to heal them of their ailment."

"Sounds like a scam," Lien said. Life near the Scab made her suspicious of dubious medical practices. "I heard some of the people of the Last Summer wrongly believed that a lot of things existed in a binary form. Like gender. Or good and evil."

"Modern duality theory has nothing to do with gender or morality. It's about cosmic material energy."

It still sounded like a scam. "How does that even work?"

"Some people used to believe that the human body had a number of 'yang' organs, like the stomach, and 'yin' organs, like kidneys, and harmonious balance between the elements were needed for good health. This aspect of duality theory no longer holds water in modern medical theory, but modern Injunct treatment is itself based on one such study of the duality, one that people once called 'acupuncture'. It's possible that our ancestors also learned how to purposefully disrupt the balance. And in so doing, disrupt reality itself." Servertu waved at the rinse.

"And you think the Room is the key to that?" Lien asked doubtfully. She couldn't quite draw a line from Injunct surgery to something like the Rinse.

"The world's out of balance. Especially in places close to hot Change."

"If low ebb disturbs you, high ebb's going to be a bitch," Lien told Yusuf.

Yusuf looked shaken. "The shared hallucination thing is true? Everyone sees what you're seeing?"

"Yah."

Yusuf glanced away towards the thorns. His hooves skittered on the dirt, nervous again. "There're some things in my past…" He trailed off as Lien let out a sharp bark of laughter.

"There're skeletons in everyone's past, halfer. Duality theory or whatever you're here for, I don't care. I'm here for the money and you're both here for… some weird purpose or other. I don't care what you see about me, and you shouldn't care what I see about you."

Yusuf said nothing. His glance towards Servertu said volumes enough. "Right," Yusuf said finally, when Servertu didn't seem to notice.

"I'm stuck here with the two of you, I know that. I won't run off and leave you just because I see something in your past," Lien said, growing irritated. Fine time for Yusuf to finally get twitchy.

"Right," Yusuf said again. He looked at Servertu again, biting his lip.

"Besides, distortion isn't the worst thing you can get at the Rinse. I'll take the live replay of my life, or yours, or Servertu's anytime. Over everything else that could happen." Lien gestured at her Changed body.

Yusuf pawed at the ground. "Hallucinations and time distortions and those ghosts." There was a loathing that drenched the usual flat edge of his voice. "Changer."

Despite Lien's dire predictions, the Rinse remained at low ebb even into the evening. They reached an asphalt path that cut through thorn and scrub, a narrow route up a steep slope. The safehouse was the lobby of an apartment block, the top four stories long damaged and open to the elements. The walls on the upper eastern side had been shorn away at an inexplicable angle. Other buildings around the apartment block were stumps and piles of brick and rust. Clear lines of sight.

Like all of Raahi's safehouses, this one was combi-locked. Or it should have been. The lockpad was a blackened crater, the door blasted aside. Someone from within had blockaded the door with a table, turned upright to close off the door save for a thin wedge of darkness at the top. Lien shoved experimentally at the table. Didn't budge.

"Changer's hairy godsdamned *balls*." Lien closed her eyes as she tried to recalculate her location. If they moved back to the Rinse at this time of day—

Yusuf turned and struck the table squarely with his hind feet. Lien yelped. His force rocked the table back a fraction.

"Stop that," Lien hissed. She looked around wildly.

"Someone's in there," Yusuf said.

Lien edged away to a side, away from the barricaded door. "How'd you know that?"

"The table. Look at the way it's been pushed. It's half again as wide as the door, but it's been pushed flush, with things piled behind it," Servertu said.

"If you're right, you're assuming that whoever's in there is going to be friendly. Not halfway on the way to becoming a ghulkin or a Crow?"

"Dar Lien?" The voice behind the door was weak. "Lien?"

Lien exchanged a wary look with Servertu and Yusuf. "Who's there?"

"You don't—" Someone coughed wetly, as though hacking up a dollop of something sticky. "I'm Cheung. Remember? Three runs back?"

"Beaker Johnny?"

"That's right," Cheung whispered. The Cheung Lien remembered had what Raahi called a parade-ground voice. No volume control—he'd been forbidden from speaking during a run unless necessary. If this was Cheung, something had reached into his voicebox and torn it to shreds. "We did a thirteen person job with Raahi. Lost two on the way out to psychons."

"What are you doing here? Alone?" Lien asked.

Cheung coughed again. "Got… left behind. Ghulkin packs rushed us a day back. Hella lot of them." Another coughing fit, then a long silence punctuated by soft groans. "Survey Team got separated. Didn't survive. I ran out here. Thought... thought maybe I could do what you did before. Make it out on the edge of the hot Change."

Cheung had been muscle. Lien hardly talked to the muscle. Next to scouts, they had the highest death rate. She didn't like to get attached. Lien wouldn't have told Cheung that she regretted what she had done. Better to die in the Scab than delay her death sentence. "I shouldn't have survived what I did. Cheung, are you... how are you—"

"I'm turning ghulkin, I think?" Cheung said, matter-of-fact to the last. Like any Scab veteran. "Not pretty. Give myself maybe four more hours or so. Not sure. I thought... I thought I'd just Change, but I'm pretty sure I'm turning into ghulkin. My arms, they're... And I'm losing my hair. Skin's gone orange."

"Can you still move the stuff out of the way?"

"Sorry. Can barely crawl. Whoever you've got with you was doing a fine job of breaking it down. Have at it."

Lien looked towards Servertu. "Something wrong?" Servertu asked, lowering his voice.

"Do you have anything that could fix Cheung? Tech? You can take it out of my pay," Lien whispered back.

"Friend of yours?"

"Acquaintance. But..." Lien trailed off. She barely knew Cheung, but he was here. Still human. And Lien knew precious few people anyway, outside of Raahi's runs. Her inconstant version of family.

"If he's somehow bypassing the Changeling stage and turning into ghulkin, he's too far gone. We can ease him on his way, if that is what he prefers," Servertu said.

Lien stared down at her Changed legs, the unlovely multi-jointed edges of them, the spindly forms. "All right. Break the door down. We'll ask."

CHAPTER SEVEN

"Sorry," Cheung said apologetically, all the way to the end when Lien had cut his throat. "Sorry."

They buried him out around the back of the safehouse, in what had once been the apartment's ground floor flat's garden. It was walled in, with a partially collapsed awning that hid it from most of the sky. The ground was dry but soft enough to dig up with a spade that Servertu found in a tiny shed. They piled debris over the body just in case. Ghulkin sometimes dug up corpses where they could. Afterwards, Lien washed her hands and arms clean with what was left of Cheung's water. It was a waste of water in the Scab, but neither Yusuf nor Servertu said anything as she scrubbed her skin out over the garden. Where she had ended Cheung's life.

Yusuf was barricading them back in with the same table. It had splintered a little but hadn't shattered when he had kicked it aside. As Yusuf stacked the crates he'd pushed away back behind it, Servertu made dinner. Lien forced herself to eat. She swallowed gulps of hot soup without tasting it.

"First time?" Yusuf asked, when Lien was helping Servertu wipe down and clean up.

"Yusuf," Servertu protested.

"No," Lien said, a little defensively. "Third. It never gets easier."

"Good. Once it does, you're better off leaving the business."

"That's what I've been told." At Servertu's questioning stare, Lien said, "Out in a run, everyone's got to rely on everyone. You're family when the run starts until the end. Anyone who's just out for themselves is a liability. You can count on them to give up when the going gets bad."

Servertu blinked owlishly. "Not what I've heard about runners."

"A lot of what you've heard about runners is probably true. People who'd willingly go back into the Changelands over and over aren't exactly sensible," Lien said, with a wry twist to her mouth.

"On the contrary, you're one of the most sensible people I have ever met," Servertu told her. "And you're kind. A kind person."

"Sensible people don't follow the Rinse out of the Scab."

"You survived."

"I shouldn't have survived." Lien put her hand into her pocket. Touched the edge of the photograph. She drew it out to look at it, trying to figure out what unnerved her so much about it. It wasn't that it was the Room. Lien had seen it enough in her dreams. She still did, even as she remembered nothing else from that time in her life.

It wasn't the steel operating bench off to the side. Or the black stains on the white tiles. The computer screens were dark, with data in blue streams that were as unreadable on the photograph as they were in her dreams. To the right was part of a tall steel storage unit, air-sealed. Little rows of glass vials within. Front and centre on the bottom edge of the photograph was a set of feet. Children's feet, as though the person taking the photograph was looking out through the child's eyes.

"This is impossible," Lien said. She held up the photograph. "It's exactly the same as my dream."

"Yes, it is." Servertu nodded. Lien didn't miss how Yusuf started to tense up.

"How?"

"There are others with the same vision of the day of their Change-infection. Their 'death', as you in the Changelands like to call it."

"Other survivors of the Room."

"That's right. They know this image. They've seen it before, in its exact detail. In the Archives, we know of five others. You're the sixth."

"Five others with the same dream? Not possible." Lien repeated, astonished and off-balance. She didn't know what to make of Servertu's assertion.

"It is what it is," Servertu said wearily.

"How many like me have you met so far? In person?"

"Two. But neither were… held in circumstances that made conversation useful."

"What circumstances?"

"One was in Selangor when it was overrun. Died before my eyes. The other was in the Bakgut Plains, but he was quite mad by the time Yusuf and I located him. Still, he was lucid enough to give us a general idea of the Room's location."

"He knew about me?"

"Not of you. He knew that the Room was in the City within the Scab."

"Then how did you know about me? What's in the Room? Why was I there?"

"That's what I've tried for a while to have answered."

"But—"

Servertu raised a palm. "Bear with me for a moment. So. What we know in the Archives is this. At some point in the past, humanity began to fight wars over resources. Particularly clean water. Widespread environmental degradation created vast wastelands, like the Scablands. The urban sprawl degenerated. Points of civilisation tended to gather into large cities. Megacities that would eventually become places like the Citadel and Kandan."

Lien nodded slowly. Out in Basa'at, there hadn't been much space or time to speculate about the history before the world had died. Nobody could read and there were no schools outside the Quarantined Cities anyway. She'd heard theories during runs. That the Gods had grown angry. Or that the Changer-God had eaten them to become the God of the Dead. That the world herself had grown tired of men and risen up to curse them with plagues. Raahi had never been interested in the theories. Nor had Lien. Theories wouldn't fill her belly. Stop her Change.

"The wars caused the period known as the Last Summer. City

fought city and destroyed each other. In the end, some Cities allied together to make a final weapon. Something went wrong and caused the Change. The Cities within the zones now known as the Scab, the Bakgut Plains, Selangor, Subterra, Delha, and Nanhai." Servertu ticked them off on his fingers.

"Six zones," Lien said. She narrowed her eyes. "Six people who have the same dream."

"Yes. The same impression of the point of their death."

"One in the Bakgut Plains, one in Selangor. Me over in the Scab." Lien continued, frowning. "Are the rest…?"

"Not so neatly, no. I couldn't find the others. It's possible that the numerical parallel is a coincidence. That they're not paired with various zones."

"Whatever they were. Whatever I am."

"Lien—"

"I don't believe you," Lien said abruptly. "This is ridiculous."

"I've given you the image."

"Which you won't explain," Lien said, knowing that her voice was rising. Yusuf's hand was straying idly to the stock of his rifle. She didn't care. "Nothing about this makes sense!"

"I know what it sounds like. And I don't expect you to believe any of it. All I want is to find the Room. And perhaps a little closure for you as well," Servertu said gently.

"I'm going to sit in the garden." Lien crabbed away, clenching her hands. She crumpled the colourstat in her fist. Her feet crunched into the dry gravel, taking her to the pile of debris that marked Cheung's new grave. Lien stared hard at it. Took in a soft breath and shoved the piece of paper back into her jacket.

Lien had always wondered why she had died so young, a death that had given her claws for hands. Had her family left her in the hospice, perhaps, hoping for a cure? Lien had always told herself that this was the case. That they hadn't expected the final airstrikes to come so soon. That they would have come to see her again during visiting hours, horrific as the hospice's conditions had been. In the ruins of the City and the riots from the hot Change that had come, Lien had not been the only orphan to escape. Not the only orphan to stagger into Basa'at.

The chill started to creep in. Lien wrapped her clawed hands over her arms as Yusuf stepped out into the small garden beside her. He had to pull his hat off to duck under the ruined awning, bending forward. His hair was an unruly mess of thick black waves. Yusuf pushed his goggles down to his neck. Under them, his eyes were dark and narrow. UnChanged. In the gloom, he looked like a myth-walker, with his tall war-made body drawn in powerful lines, with his fierce-edged face. Yusuf wore the easy cruelty of his innate strength with an indifference that Lien envied.

"Doing all right?" Yusuf asked quietly.

"Surprised."

"Servertu's like that. Don't take it personally."

"Are rich people from the Citadel all like that?"

"That's not what he is. He's an academic. Lots of them are like that. They've been living in the Archives so long that it's hard to deal with people."

"I'm not angry with him."

"That's good," Yusuf said, with a carefully even tone. Yusuf had been prepared for temper.

Lien glanced behind her. Servertu was curled up against the saddlebags, asleep. She lowered her tone. "How'd you meet him?"

Yusuf shot her a guarded look. "Archives put an ad out for a minder, I applied. Money was good."

"You let him put a saddle on you."

"Wasn't him. More efficient this way. I'd rather know exactly where he is than have him ride something that might bolt at the wrong stimuli."

"Or he could walk." Lien grinned sharply.

"Leave him to walk and he'll walk off a cliff without noticing it, reading all the way. Faster this way. We go at my pace."

"How long have the two of you been travelling together?"

"Quite a while," Yusuf said, evasive.

Long enough for Servertu to be more than just an employer to Yusuf. "I'm surprised you're still at it. Babysitting someone through Changelands. Is the money that good?" Lien asked, deliberately misunderstanding. Another guarded glance. She couldn't make out what colour Yusuf's eyes were when it was this dark out, but Lien could read the wariness set into the lines of Yusuf's face.

"Money's good," Yusuf said finally.

"You believe him? About people with the same dream? A special Room?"

"Seen things that are hard to believe in the Changelands," Yusuf said, after a long pause. "Not sure what's possible and not possible anymore. I'm just here as the muscle."

"Scouts have to have a bit more imagination than that," Lien said, if lightly.

Yusuf tugged his goggles back up with a grunt. "Get some sleep."

"I will. I just want to sit out here with Beaker for a while."

"Thought he was just an acquaintance."

"I still knew him. I *killed* him," Lien said, her tone edged. It wasn't Cheung, though. She just wanted to be alone for a while. Yusuf nodded curtly, ducking back under the low doorway.

The morning was crisp, the air unusually clean. Lien breathed deeply as they edged out from behind the newly moved table. They'd found an old cache of what Servertu called 'newspapers' in one of the cupboards before breakfast, and he'd been poring over them since, barely pausing to climb onto Yusuf's back.

"This one was printed two days before the Change. Couple of months before the prefab riots," Servertu said. The newspapers were too bulky to fit into the saddlebags as a whole and had to be left behind. Servertu had kept a set, opening it wide before him as Yusuf started to walk.

"What riots?" Lien asked. The few prefabs she knew were a wary bunch of drifters, never staying long.

"Prefab tech became popular in the final year or so of the Last Summer. It was all medical before. Prosthetics and such. Then it became military. Enhanced people, hybrid organic computer processing, weapons. In the end, it became more public. Became a fad if you could afford it, especially for the young and rich. Sparked off the so-called Humanist Riots. At what level does a prefab stop being a human, and so on."

"That's ridiculous," Lien said, conscious of Yusuf's presence so close by. "Prefabs are human. So what if they have to swap out a bit or two?"

"The general consensus was that quarter prefabs were fine, especially if it was a medical matter. But halfers and three quarts were not. Riots on all sides." Servertu raised the broadsheet to make a point. There was a photo on it of a car burning, someone frozen mid-throw. "Sadly, even though it's been decades since, the impression remains. Especially in the Changelands. The Citadel's rather more forgiving. Particularly once people realized prefab parts aren't affected by the Change and started using it as a viable medical alternative to invasive injuncts."

Lien bristled, defensive. "Usually, if you meet a prefab out in the Changelands, it isn't a medical thing. They're either from some militant group or somebody who thinks that modding in tiger parts will give him a bigger dick."

"Yusuf said you didn't have an opinion," Servertu said.

"I'm Changed enough to view prefab tech differently. And I run a provision shop in a nowhere town. Customers are customers. Besides. So far as I've seen, the halfer you've got with you isn't completely useless. Scout's opinion." Lien winked at Yusuf.

Yusuf snorted. His shoulders relaxed as Servertu let out a startled laugh. "Yusuf's very competent. I'm lucky to have him."

"I hope you pay him well," Lien said.

"Pay?" Servertu blinked.

"We're close to the thorns," Yusuf said, raising his voice a fraction. "Are we crossing back down to the banks?"

Lien stared at Yusuf, but he remained impassive. She pointed. "See that building over there? Series of long concrete chimneys? That's near our next safehouse. Last one before we reach the City proper."

"Old power station," Servertu squinted into the distance. "The Aljyun District?"

"Used to be a slum. According to Raahi."

Yusuf grunted. "Those places tend to be full of mutates. Last places to get evacuated. Or treated."

"Not where we're going. Hopefully. But on the bright side, maybe your friend Serverun's taken care of that already. Looking at where the Crow cloud is, I think he's probably about to cross into the City right now." Lien gestured at the distant specks.

Servertu closed his eyes. "Cross into the… Bridging, right? That's what it's called."

"You guys did your research." Good. Lien didn't like to explain Bridging procedure to newcomers. It was something she usually left to Raahi. "He'll need a whole day for that. To be safe. You can only Bridge on low ebb, preferably around midday. If they miss the window, they got to wait."

"Unless he's no longer interested in being safe," Servertu said.

"Any guide he bought who's worth his salt would tell him it's suicide to Bridge out of a window. Would refuse to let him."

"Serverun doesn't often like to listen, unfortunately." Servertu's expression took on a pinched look.

"That's good for you if he doesn't Bridge properly. His expedition will be mostly screwed. We'll catch up," Lien said.

"Mostly?"

"Well, they won't all make it across. If they even try." If it was Raahi leading the pack, he'd flat out refuse to Bridge out of window. Serverun would've had to go at it alone.

"They don't all need to make it across," Servertu said. He looked even grimmer.

"That's beyond reckless. Suicidal. Why would Serverun want to rush? Does he even know that you're here?"

"He'll want to rush." Servertu carefully folded up the broadsheet and fitted it into Yusuf's pack. "And yes, he probably does know that I'm here."

Lien frowned at Servertu, inoffensive-looking Servertu with his fussy airs and his solemn face. She tried to imagine a well-armed contingent rushing a sup run just because its leader knew that Servertu was in the vicinity. "And that worries him?"

"I presume it should."

Lien looked at Yusuf, who said nothing, picking his pace into a trot over the asphalt. The road they were now on hugged a cliffside, with thorns and the bank of the Rinse to their right. Ruins overhead. They were visibly alone, but Lien knew better. The closer they got to the City, the more treacherous the terrain. Ghulkin and Crows weren't the only mutates out here.

"If it's Raahi leading the run, he won't rush," Lien said. She wished she felt more confident about that. "Unless. Does Serverun have your prototype? Can he give people immunity to the Rinse?"

"Probably. We should hurry."

CHAPTER EIGHT

Mid-ebb brought with it a mirror into another land. A small city on the banks of a dead river. Traces of its previous life were everywhere: vaulted districts expanded as fallen leaves outwards from the dried docks. White fingered piers were sunk as fossilized teeth into bleached sand. "Yaran," Yusuf said curtly.

"Where you were born?" Lien asked. Yusuf ignored her, turning his face away.

The piers swept into concrete rooms. Steel gurneys and racks of tools, vat-grown spliced fab parts still floating in their jars. The glass silos were overlaid in a translucent sheen over the shells of tightly-packed structures, once homes for the poorest in the city that was. Subsidized blocks of unlovely flats sat intact in the Aljyun District, blocky and sun-stained and dark. Even the psychons left this part of the Scab untouched. An unrelenting misery clung to the brickwork, ingrained even before the Change.

Over the Rinse, the window into Yaran flickered. The concrete rooms were full. People in coats and masks and gloves sped apart. Children were being strapped down to gurneys and wheeled away. Buckets were carried back into view, full to the brim with gristle and parts. There were people whose job was just to wash the floor with hoses and mops. Lien wasn't sure why they even bothered. By the time they worked a corner of a room to the next, the tiles were bloody again.

"Changer," Lien whispered. "That... is that all true?"

Yusuf flinched as Servertu rested a hand on his flank, but he looked straight ahead instead of answering. "I'm afraid so," Servertu said softly. "Oh, Yusuf."

Lien raised her jointed body up as far as it could go, vestigial spines quivering. She dug multi-kneed legs into the rock for purchase. "I'm sorry."

"Don't be. Came out luckier than most. Alive," Yusuf said.

"You were kidnapped?"

"No. Orphanage offset costs by sending problem kids to prefab clinics. Yaran's a prefab tech town. Lots of competition, what with other prefab towns close by."

Lien tried not to watch, but she couldn't turn from the Rinse. The window flickered. Someone masked and in a doctor's white coat was keying something into a console. The viewpoint skewed wildly as prefab men with carapaced arms strapped limbs onto an operating table, angling a mirror overhead. It was Yusuf as a child, already missing his left leg, the stump tightly wrapped in bloody bandages. His mouth was open in a soundless scream. Guiltily, Lien felt grateful that mid-ebb had no sound. "That's horrible."

"They needed to innovate by experimenting." Yusuf sounded indifferent.

Lien blanched, dragging her stare away from the Rinse-sight. "Changer's balls."

"Didn't get off too bad."

"They just... let you go?"

"Got loose." Yusuf said. He relaxed when Servertu patted his flank.

Rinse-sight ebbed, turning into nothing more than a shimmer of hot Change. They walked through the morning, settling into the shade of a wall during a break for lunch. A twisted wire fence sat around an old concrete yard dotted with debris. The brick wall that lined two of its flanks was scrawled thickly over with old paint, tags over tags.

"Did you kill them?" Lien asked as Servertu slipped off Yusuf's back to stretch his legs.

"Got to be specific. Killed a lot of people," Yusuf said.

Lien didn't back down. "Them. The people in the labs. The ones who gave you a horse half with fancy spinework."

"Pretty good job." Yusuf swished his shortened tail. "I was probably thirteen tops when it was done. They tried other parts first that didn't take. Was dying when they stitched me up into a colt half that did. Wanted to see if the prefab work would grow as I grew. Revolutionary stuff."

"Looks like it worked?"

Servertu shot Yusuf a worried stare, but he looked away when Yusuf merely shrugged. "Got lucky. Gene splicing in the horse bit worked out right. Spines were a leftover graft that also took. Some of the other kids who got out, not so much. Bird halves where the prefab half had a bird's lifespan. Insect halves that rotted right off in days. Like I said. Lucky."

"Hope you killed them." Lien bowed her head, concentrating on her ration bar. "That day in Basa'at. Sorry I said that you got the spines for fun."

"Not what you said. And it's okay. You meant well."

After lunch, as Lien cleared up, Servertu walked over to the tangled mouth of the fenced gap, looking out past the car park towards one of the squat blocks of brick and concrete flats beyond. His hood was drawn back, hands folded behind his back. Yusuf's tail twitched, visibly fighting the urge to corral Servertu back into the shade. Servertu's eyes were distant, studying a set of calculus that only he could see.

"How many people?" Servertu murmured.

"What?" Lien asked.

"Living in those." Servertu waved at the flats.

"None. Obviously no psychons here. Just ghulkin."

Servertu's expression tightened briefly, as though Lien had said the wrong thing. "Strange. That they aren't venturing out. The ghulkin."

"It's still daylight."

"We were attacked by a pack in daylight," Servertu reminded her.

"Maybe that group we met earlier on was a fluke." So Lien hoped.

"They're all adapting. Strange how those closest to the Rinse seem to be adapting less quickly." Servertu shaded his eyes.

Yusuf shuddered, eyeing the darkened holes of windows with distaste. "Maybe they became something else. I haven't seen any movement."

"Exactly," Servertu said encouragingly. Lien's heart sank. She was starting to recognise that tone.

"We're not going to check," Lien said.

"You aren't. I am." Servertu gestured at the closest building. "There's a fire escape built along the flank. I'll climb up, look through some of the windows. That's all."

"Servertu," Yusuf protested.

"I have a feeling about this place," Servertu said.

Yusuf was unimpressed. "Good or bad feeling?"

"We have to catch up with Serverun, don't we? This is a distraction." Lien said, surprised by Servertu's insistence. She tried to follow his gaze. Had he seen something she hadn't?

"Stay here. It'll only take a minute," Servertu said.

"I'll go too," Lien volunteered reluctantly. "I don't hear the ghulkin."

"*Servertu*," Yusuf said.

"Stay here."

Yusuf watched anxiously from the foot of the fire escape as Servertu and Lien navigated the rusty ladder, then the narrow flights of steps. Servertu occasionally stopped to peer into a window before taking notes. Each time, Lien tensed up, expecting ghulkin to burst out at any moment. She was clammy with sweat by the time they made it to the top floor. Servertu stiffened at the look of something through the window. Lien looked.

She wished she didn't. Flinching violently back, Lien nearly fell right off the steps. She bit at the wrist of her claw to stifle her cry as Servertu pressed a hand on her shoulder to steady her. Within the room was a huge, fleshy lump, rippled with grey fingertips, expanding and contracting as a diaphragm.

Whatever it was, it stayed within the building. Servertu made a few quick notes, shooting the lump a lingering stare before heading back down the fire escape. Lien followed, relieved. Floor by floor, again anticipating an attack. Yusuf had backed off to give himself and his rifle a better line of sight. He was dancing with impatience by the time Servertu got to the ground floor.

"The ghulkin nearer to the Change are experiencing a far more accelerated mutation," Servertu said.

"Changer." Lien landed on the dirt with a faint thump, pale.

"What was that? All that? It's not becoming a Crow!"

Servertu climbed onto Yusuf's back. "I've always suspected that Crows and other large mutates are aggregate versions of the ghulkin. The incubation form we saw in that room is highly suggestive. Many smaller life forms, mutating together to form larger ones. That's why Crows and large creatures like the Mighal shake off seemingly grievous injuries. They have multiple organ copies, functioning together as a whole."

Lien shuddered. As she tried to swallow a wave of nausea, Yusuf said, "Guess that's why Crows and Mighal are so much bigger than ghulkin."

"Exactly. And the Mighal, which are bigger than Crows, are more formless. A giant mouth on feet, effectively. That thing up there is even less defined. If only we had the time to study the incubation stage more closely."

Lien swallowed more nausea. "Thank the Changer for small mercies."

"Don't see Crows outside the Scab. Anything bigger than Crows here?" Yusuf asked.

"Never seen anything bigger than a Crow."

"Not yet," Servertu predicted.

Lien pulled a face. "We're *so* going to get eaten by a giant monster blob." No one laughed.

The old power station was on the edge of the Aljyun District. It was inland away from the Rinse, within sight of the great spans of rusted girders that made up the Bridge. They paused for a moment on a rising arc of concrete, jammed bumper to bumper with vehicles of varying shapes and sizes. Any bodies had long been dragged away for food, any fuel and useful parts scavenged. The vehicles remained empty, silent monuments an ancient panic.

The Bridge squatted like a giant, narrow spiderweb of metal cabling, strung between the mainland of the Scab and the City over the Rinse. The only way in that hadn't been warped to nothing. It sat high enough over the Rinse that its topmost layer of concrete was out of the hot Change, but the Change was slowly eating away the layer beneath, gradually but surely twisting the Bridge apart. The top layer of concrete was broken into rippled crusts, the cabling and the layer beneath it already having melted together into fantastical shapes. The Change twisted even the man-made bones of cities in its image.

"He tried to Bridge," Lien said, pointing. There was a new wreck in the centre of the Bridge, still visible under dying light. Crows were perched on it in a feeding frenzy, tearing at bodies and occasionally stabbing at each other with their huge beaks. "Maybe that's all of them."

"Doubt it. Flattened vehicles over there. Someone got away," Yusuf said.

Lien shook her head, torn between disgust and awe. "It's suicidal to force a crossing. If the Rinse is at high ebb, the Bridge's dangerous."

"He's desperate," Servertu said. Lien readied an objection, sure that Servertu was going to insist on Bridging even in the dying light. Thankfully, he said nothing of the sort. "We'll find a place to rest. Bridge during the next window."

"Gonna be hard. If the Crows hang around." It had been years and Lien still couldn't predict the Crows. Sometimes they ate their fill and flew off. Sometimes they lingered and fought each other to the death.

"We'll have to chance it," Servertu said.

"What's the danger with Bridging out of window?" Yusuf asked, following Lien through narrow channels left to him on the road. Some of the cars were parked close enough that the hot metal pressed against his flanks. From how tense Yusuf looked, he was probably constantly fighting the urge to bolt. His hands were clenched on the stock of his rifle.

"Something warps Rinse-sight on the Bridge. Cross when it's too hot and your mind shatters. Or you'd disappear. Or jump. Seen all three happen."

"You've crossed out of window?" Yusuf asked.

"Nah. But even at low ebb, sometime's there'd be accidents. That's why you've got to take your time to cross. Slowly. Watching the ebb. It's unstable on the Bridge. Doesn't ebb high or low all at once. Just at parts."

"A skipping game," Servertu said, near inaudible. Yusuf

angled his head to look back at his master, but Servertu's hood was pulled low over his face. The road angled deeper into blocks of low-rise buildings, blocking their view of the Bridge. Lien scuttled ahead, alert for ghulkin or psychons. The buildings were quiet, just like the Aljyun District had been. Something wasn't right. Even here, the world shouldn't be so empty.

The path led to a yard gated off by a high wire fence, too high for ghulkin to climb over. It was reinforced with tied-on scrap metal. The original gate was padlocked shut, blocked from the back with the flank of an old truck. The yard's cars had been arranged into neat lines. Ribs on a funnel. Anything that broke through the gate would have to go through a corridor overlooked by narrow windows from the high concrete towers of the old power station. Against one of the windows, there was a brief gleam of something silvery. Lien swore quietly under her breath.

"We move on?" Yusuf asked.

"I don't know where else we could go for the night that could be safe. Let me think."

"Aljyun District'?"

"With those weird mutates in the rooms?" Lien shuddered.

"We can block up an empty room. And those later stage mutates weren't moving. If we're quiet, maybe we can avoid notice," Servertu said.

Lien glared at the old power station as though it had personally betrayed her. "Fine. We turn back. Find someplace intact."

"Should've expected it. Earlier safehouse had one of your friends," Yusuf said.

Lien bit down her temper. Shouting at Yusuf wasn't going to help. Worse, it might call down a Crow. "We're not getting in the usual way anyway. Some asshole blocked off the gate."

Yusuf held up a hand. Lien jerked her stare back to the old power station. From a small service door that led into the station, a man was coming out, arms upraised. Yusuf backed away slowly. Lien craned her head forward as the man got closer. Tall man with powerfully built shoulders, no skin visible under the sand-coloured jacket and khaki breeches. A shotgun was slung across his back. Black goggles could be seen under the scarf that wrapped around his face, and he had a combat knife strapped to a thigh, a belt of pouches slung low over his hips.

The stranger stopped walking at the first line of cover, hands still up. "That you, Lien?" he called. His deep, familiar voice was all sharp consonants.

"Sure is. Changer's bloody balls, Raahi. Fancy seeing you here," Lien said warily.

Raahi grinned at her. He was relaxed, his bulk uneven under the jacket. Sign of a thorough and very professional Injunct. Comfortable and relaxed even this deep in the Scablands. Raahi dropped his hands. Yusuf tensed up, but Raahi merely hooked his thumbs into his belt.

"Got new friends," Raahi said, with a nod at Yusuf.

"So do you. I'm hurt. You didn't ask me along." Lien said.

"Wasn't a salvage run." Raahi spat on the ground. "Got picked up in Jinsha'an. Offer I couldn't refuse. Didn't have time to swing by Basa'at or I would've. Bossman wanted to rush."

"Armed party bulling all the way through, Bridging out of window, that your idea?"

"First bit yeah. Second bit, no. I'm here, aren't I? Told the Bossman, Bridging out of a window's suicide. Wasn't in this for killing myself. He paid up half what I was owed and I stood down with some of the boys. Rest of the muscle decided to head through." Raahi spat again. "Reckless bastards."

"Didn't expect that to happen?"

"I did the run on condition that I was leading the damned run. Worked fine up till now. On the other hand, I think we've done enough damage to the psychons that our next salvage run will be a walk in the park. Bossman rolls with an army like I've never seen. Saboteurs, snipers, everything."

Raahi pulled down his scarf, though not his goggles, revealing a long, lupine face that was all hard angles. Jutting cheekbones and a sharp-edged brow beneath a shaved dome of a skull, curved nose set over a narrow mouth. It was an unlovely face and a hard one, but at least it was a familiar one. Lien couldn't help but feel reassured. Even if it was clear from the gleam at the windows that they were being marked from the power station.

"So you're heading out? Cutting your losses?" Lien asked.

"Not really. Since we're here, and since we got only part of the pay, I think we'll do a salvage run. On the quiet. Gonna Bridge properly tomorrow. You and your friends can come with. We can work out a split."

"What about your Bossman?"

"Him? Damned if I know. We've been paid out. He don't bother us, we don't bother him."

"I got my own Bossman right now," Lien said apologetically, gesturing at Yusuf and Servertu. "And I know about you and halfers."

"Got some halfers in back," Raahi jerked his thumb over at the power station. "Can't be choosers on a rushed run. I don't like halfers. Doesn't mean I stab them on sight."

Lien looked over to Yusuf. He started to shake his head. She didn't blame him. Changer knew it was ripe for a setup, an ambush.

"All right," Servertu said.

Raahi laughed, gruff and hoarse. "I'll get the crew to roll out the welcome, then. C'mon in. We should talk."

CHAPTER NINE

"Beaker didn't make it," Lien said. Raahi had decided to share supplies. Generous gesture in the Scab, even if it was obvious from the pullcart of boxes that they'd come with resources to spare. Military-grade rations too, heartier than even the soup rations Servertu was carrying.

Raahi nodded. They ate perched on the mezzanine walkway. Raahi's legs were dangling out into space, Lien's folded beneath her. Yusuf and Servertu were in a corner, eating and talking quietly to themselves. "Sorry to hear."

"That why you had your crew block off the gate?" It had taken all the prefabs in Raahi's crew to move the truck, and they'd moved it back once Lien and the others had been let through.

"Yeah. How in Changer did you make it this far with just those two? Or did you lose your own crew?"

"Nope. Was just us."

Raahi raised his eyebrows. "Got to be some story."

"We followed your dust. Your people did a serious number on the psychons. We passed a lot of empty watchtowers. Even Aljyun was empty."

Raahi grunted. He glanced back down at Yusuf. "That's Yaran work if I know it."

"Makes a difference?"

"Look at the other halfers. Any of their stapled-on bits work as seamlessly to you? I know you think I'm prejudiced, not liking prefabs. Thing is, I got reasons. Most of them we see out here don't last. They go wrong in the head or in their bodies or both. Prefab work doesn't always take. Or if it does, it often rots out.

Poisons the brain."

"He didn't have a choice. Rinse-sight showed me. That's how Yaran got so good. They practiced on kids nobody wanted. He was from an orphanage."

The play for sympathy didn't work. "Looks like it worked out just fine for him. What did his boss offer you?"

So Raahi had guessed that Yusuf was just the muscle. "Taels. What else?"

"Hope you didn't sell out for cheap."

Lien scowled at him. "You've got some nerve saying that to me. Given you didn't even take me on this run. Rush or no rush."

He raised his palms. "Hey, you made it here. Babysitting them. By yourself. You deserve a lot more than what you'd get from a sup run. That's what I meant."

Was Raahi planning on robbing her? The taelstick in her inner vest felt like it was pressing against her warped ribs. "None of your business."

"Calm down, Dar. If you need a reference for Injuncts or something, I can help you. Not out of the kindness of my heart. You're a good scout. Hate to lose you."

"You're such a darling, thanks."

"It's a bad way to go."

"I know. I was there for Cheung. Wonder what happened? You usually run a tight ship."

Raahi looked over the mezzanine level to the posted watch by the windows. "Okay. I confess. I've never done a run like this before. Muscling in, shock and awe. Never done a run where I wasn't the boss either. I made mistakes. We had a bad skirmish, Cheung and some guys got separated from the pack."

"Didn't think to go back for him?"

"You know the rules."

Lien bit down her retort. Everyone who ran with Raahi knew his rules. If you got separated, you either signalled your position or tried to catch up. Raahi didn't like wasting time looking for stragglers. And he didn't wait long. "Right."

"I didn't want to do it this way. Rushing in with an army and APCs. I told the Bossman, what's the hurry? Even if it wasn't off-peak for sup runs, there've been teams going in and out of the City for years, and I haven't heard of anybody finding some secret Room."

Lien's claws curled against her bowl, the sharp tips tinkling against fibreglass. She was all too aware that Raahi was watching her closely. As were some of the prefabs down below. "Neither have I. Not my problem. All those two want to do is make it into the City. I get paid, we get out. And sure. Put me in touch with someone who can do a good Injunct."

"You'd be looking at Kandan, not the Citadel. I know someone there who's cutting edge. He doesn't just freeze the Change in someone, he can even reverse bits of it. Hurts like a bitch and the end result ain't pretty, but it works." Raahi pulled off his left glove, revealing a gnarled hand with whorls of greyish scar tissue. It was unmistakably human. The last time Lien had seen his palm, it had been bound against a splint, slowly turning into a flipper. "Doctor August Tang. Clinic's in the marina. Tell him I sent you."

"That's not prefab?"

"Nope." Raahi pulled up his sleeve. The whorls faded into browned skin, seamless. "So you see. We can help each other."

Lien tried to hide her astonishment. "What do you mean?"

Raahi chuckled. "You're in a mood. All I'm saying is, I've got a Bossman, you've got a Bossman. Both of them want in to the City. If there's trouble, I reckon we both sit it out. Keep our heads down, do a sup run. Once we're out, I'll go to Kandan with you if you want. If you're being paid what you're worth, once you get all fixed up, you could probably afford to settle down in Kandan. Meet someone, start a family—"

Lien sniffed loudly. "No thanks." She had never had any interest in romance or in sex, and had always been most comfortable with her own company.

Over in Yusuf's corner, Servertu was curling up to sleep over the saddlebags. Yusuf met Lien's eyes, expressionless. He looked away first, his tail swishing. Restless, maybe. Yusuf and his perfectly fitted prefab parts, immune to the Change. Servertu, who was completely UnChanged. Sheer envy made the rations sit heavily in her gut. She pushed it down. Lien might be ambivalent about Yusuf and unnerved by Servertu but they had saved her life at least once so far. Out on the Scab, you remembered your debts. "That's all you want from me?" Lien asked. "Bridge in together, then leave those two to their own devices?"

"Yeah."

"I took a job. I can't just abandon them in the City."

"No one's asking you to. If they survive whatever they're doing in there, sure. Lead them out."

"And the deal's still on?" Lien asked, suspicious. She was tempted. Besides, Yusuf was more than enough security for Servertu and himself.

Raahi grinned at her. "Sure."

"I thought you got paid by your Bossman. So why do you care?"

"Because you're a good scout. And I don't want you to get yourself killed for nothing. You didn't see the firepower Serverun rolled in with. If you three go head to head with APCs, you're all going to die."

"You're afraid that Serverun will think you're in league with me and attack us all."

"That too."

That sounded more like it. Raahi might like her, but Raahi's priority was always his own skin. "Let me talk to them."

Raahi grunted, skeptical.

"Think your Bossman and mine are rivals. Yours came here with an army, mine with one halfer. You think there isn't a reason for that? They took on a Crow by themselves and won. I saw it myself."

Raahi blinked. He looked over at Yusuf, who stared evenly back at them both. "Right. It's your run."

"And Raahi? If you do something that pisses them off and doesn't get me paid, I'll remember that."

Raahi nodded. Lien finished the rest of her portion as Raahi changed the subject, talking about Kandan and Citadel politics that she cared little about. She descended to the ground level to clean and stow her bowls. Yusuf was watching her the whole time, even if his eyes weren't fixed on her back. He did look squarely at her when she approached. "Good talk?" Yusuf asked.

Lien started setting up her bedding pointedly close by. "Catching up. Wanted to know why he didn't go back for Beaker."

"He had a good reason?"

"Not really. We're going to Bridge together in the next window."

"That a good idea?"

"Probably not," Lien admitted, "but if we don't, we'll waste a day waiting for them to go first. Up to you two."

Yusuf's tail twitched. Servertu had looked asleep, but he said, without opening his eyes, "We'll Bridge tomorrow."

"Great," Yusuf said sourly.

"We stick close and don't get separated." When Yusuf merely eyed her warily, Lien said, "I'm still only holding on to a deposit."

"You guys only talked about Beaker?" Yusuf asked.

"Raahi said Serverun rolled up with an army. Don't know if they made it across. But if they did, he says he doesn't want to go near them. He'd prefer us not to either. They're equipped for a sup run, not for all-out urban warfare." Lien forced herself to look up at Yusuf's eyes, through his goggles. "And I agree."

"Conflict's probably unavoidable."

"Raahi and I can handle ourselves, but we aren't soldiers. None of these folk are."

"Raahi and you, huh." Yusuf glowered at her.

"I don't expect you to fight on our behalf. Once you get me into the City, you'll be paid," Servertu said.

"Don't I have to get you two out of the Scab?"

"I wanted a guide to the City. I didn't say anything about a return trip."

"You want to stay in the City? You'll run out of supplies... wait. You guys don't expect to survive?"

"After we Bridge, we can part ways if you wish," Servertu said. He rolled over, turning his back.

Lien looked at Yusuf, who shook his head and stayed silent. She'd failed some sort of test. Whatever it was, that was fine by her. If Lien was going to get paid sooner rather than later, so much the better.

"Why are we waiting?" Yusuf muttered. They were standing with Raahi's surviving crew within sight of the Bridge. Below, the Change was at low ebb. No Crows to be seen—they'd probably eaten their fill and left. The morning sun was a purplish blotch through wavering Rinse-sight, low as it was.

"False window. Look past the square car and the bus." Beyond the first few ranks of cars, the Change still ran hot at high ebb. "There isn't always a good window."

"What's the longest you've waited for a 'good window'?" Servertu asked.

"Four days? It was pretty bad. Psychons realized we were here. Sieged the safehouse. The leader panicked and decided to chance the Bridge at part ebb. It didn't go well." Lien gestured at her thorax. Raahi would have waited it out. Or retreated. "Never did a run without Raahi again. Until now. Technically. We go when he says it's OK to go."

She thought Yusuf would object, but he nodded instead, pulling his scarf up over his nose. Servertu started to sketch the Bridge in his book. Some of the prefabs in the band shot them the occasional uneasy glance, but no one approached with overtures. Lien didn't recognise them anyway. Raahi must have put the run together in a hell of a hurry. "Where's Fatima?" Lien asked as Raahi walked over to them. "Isn't she based in Kandan too?"

"She didn't want to come."

"Maying?"

"Neither. Why?"

"Thought they've been with you on every run. Even your earliest ones."

"This isn't a usual run," Raahi said. He made a show of shading his eyes, looking over at the Bridge. "Ready to go?"

"We're waiting," Lien said.

Something wasn't right. Lien tried not to let her tension show, but when Raahi walked away to talk to another scout, Yusuf said, "Trouble?"

"Maybe." Other than Cheung, Lien recognised no-one. Even Cheung had been relatively new: he'd been muscle on their last run and nothing more. Raahi hadn't come here with any Scab veterans. Weird.

Yusuf grunted. He had one hand held loosely close to his rifle, but he looked more relaxed than he'd been last night. "We'll stay close to you on the Bridge," Servertu said.

Lien was about to reply when Raahi whistled in a quick staccato. "That's the signal. Watch the ebb. And where you step. If you see anything on that Bridge that shouldn't be there, it probably isn't."

There were fifteen of them in total. Raahi stayed in the centre of the loose line, beside the supply carts. Lien took point with one of the scouts, a prefab with multifaceted insectoid eyes and enlarged sharp-tipped ears. Their eyes wept slow droplets of white pus that they wiped away whenever they reached their chin. Lien tried not to stare. This was why she hadn't spent money to get prefab parts to arrest her Change. Seamless prefab surgery was far more expensive than an Injunct and sometimes went wrong anyway.

"Huihui," the scout said, gesturing at themself. "Pronouns are she/her."

"Dar Lien," Lien said. "Same."

"Heard of you." Huihui looked over at Yusuf and Servertu, who didn't offer their names, then turned her chin back towards the Bridge. "Safe sight," she said.

The blessing told Lien that Huihui was a sup run veteran, even if it wasn't necessarily of the Scab. "Nothing to see," Lien said, offering a scout's traditional reply.

"Doubt that," Huihui said, though she smiled. At another staccato whistle from Raahi, she stepped forward, an arrow notched to her bow.

The concrete underfoot was warm underfoot. Good sign. The Rinse was a low enough ebb that all Lien saw past the cars on the Bridge were indistinct patterns in the air, bubbles of distortion that popped and swelled in ascending streaks. Servertu wrote notes over his knees, his lips moving noiselessly. Past the bus, Huihui paused. Around the bus, Rinse-sight was thickening. Hand-like impressions pressed against the air. Someone behind Lien cursed and was quickly shushed. Huihui glanced at Lien for confirmation. When Lien tipped her head to the side, Huihui gave the distortion a berth, taking the long way around the bus. Not ideal. The mass of cars was compressed flank to flank up to the edge of the Bridge. Climbing over one wasn't going to work with supply carts and Yusuf. They had to push. The metal groaned and scoured the air as Huihui, Lien and Yusuf pushed the most intact car out of the way and to the left, clearing a path. In the corner of her eyes, Lien could see Raahi and a few others watching the sky. Scab sight.

No Crows. It was midday by the time they made it to the centre of the Bridge. The air was still and cold, the temperature dropping with each step despite the low ebb. Not good. Huihui shot Lien a worried look that Lien returned. They called a halt, Huihui backing off to talk to Raahi. Yusuf studied the overturned APC. Its driver's door and the hatch on its top were open and stained with blood. Lien cautiously circled around for a look. From the hatch of the APC wafted a charnel stink, and the spent casings of bullets were littered over the concrete and the mouth of the hatch. Empty.

Raahi pushed over, Huihui behind him. "What's the problem?"

"Temp's weird," Lien said. She kept her voice low. No sense panicking the rest of the group.

"Ebb's low," Raahi countered.

"You know a temp drop's a tide sign."

"So we push on. And quickly. There's a cleared path." Raahi pointed at the flattened vehicles. The surviving APCs had rammed open a path through the rest of the Bridge. He stared at Lien and Huihui. When neither scout disagreed, Raahi whistled, heading back towards the carts.

"Bad call?" Yusuf asked as Lien scuttled back to them.

"Hard to say. Stay close."

It grew colder and colder yet. Their breath steamed in the air. Lien shivered, her footsteps growing sluggish. Her Changed parts didn't do well in the cold. The concrete was growing slippery. Ice drew jagged patterns over the wrecked cars to either side in elaborate crystalline lace. They passed a van with icy teeth along its scraped flank, shoved aside by something heavy. Huihui slipped with a yelp next to a twisted strut. Yusuf lunged, grabbing and steadying her by the shoulder before she bashed her head against the nearest car.

"I'll take point," Lien murmured. With multiple legs, hopefully she'd have less difficulty. Nodding and pale, Huihui backed behind her. Watching her footing, digging the tip of each segmented leg firmly into the ground before moving, the going got slower. At least the Rinse had ebbed to the lowest Lien had ever seen it. No patterns in the air, no translucent impressions. Lien looked back. Supply carts were past the halfway point now. Sun still overhead. They were making decent time, despite the ice—

"Lien, stop!"

It was Servertu. Lien stopped, one leg in midair. She started to turn to look over her shoulder and caught it—a shimmer, curved against the light. A large misshapen bubble, swelling upwards. All around her. Whatever it was, she'd nearly walked into it. Behind her, Huihui screamed.

Huihui had walked face-first into the shimmer behind Lien. She stuck fast, yelling and twisting as though it burned her and Changer but it *was*. Huihui's skin was peeling off, fastened in mid-air like a wrinkled flap on the bubble. Her compound eyes were deflating like torn waterskins, releasing a bitter stink. She wrenched free, bloody, shrieking, stumbling to the side and breaking into a run. Yusuf lunged over to try and catch her but his hand closed over air. With a final scream, Huihui hit the barricade hard and toppled over, pinwheeling in the air as she fell into the Rinse.

It was a long way down.

The bubble popped with a soft plosive sound. Milky fluids and skin fell to the ground and froze fast to the asphalt. Lien swallowed hard, fighting nausea. "Forward," Servertu said, breaking the stunned silence, "but slowly, please."

It took everything Lien had to take a step. The next one was easier. "I haven't seen anything like that before here," Lien said. Her voice cracked.

"We have. Selangor. Stormsign," Yusuf said. He sounded unhappy. "Starts with the bubbles. Then mist. Once the rain comes, that's it."

"The Rinse, but as a precipitate," Servertu said.

"That's what's going to happen here?" Raahi asked, falling into step beside Yusuf.

"It might. It's hard to predict. We've seen stormsign before without a storm breaking," Servertu said.

"Changer," Lien whispered, shaken. At least most of the others behind her looked similarly disturbed, muttering among themselves.

Not Raahi. He walked over the frozen gore on the ground without breaking stride. "We push on. We're nearly in the City. If we turn back now we might get caught out of window. Worse, this 'stormsign' might be everywhere."

"Your call," Lien said.

Raahi offered her a sharp smile. "Just watch your step. We're nearly out of scouts."

CHAPTER TEN

The relief was palpable once they got off the Bridge. The sky darkened as the window closed rapidly behind them. The safehouse wasn't far. Lien led them through wreck-choked streets to a walled compound with another patchwork gate. She looked through a viewing slat set into the gate and gave the all-clear signal to Raahi. No lock on the gate. Metal brought in from the outside would often fuse or warp after months in the City, which suited them fine. They used a bolt cutter to snap open the fused chains from their last visit and pushed through, chaining the gates behind the carts. The original purpose of the safehouse was a mystery to Lien, like many of the buildings in the City. There were two rusted flagpoles to the right, warped into curls at the tips. The parked cars and vehicles in the compound had fused to the concrete, glass melting into steel. The brick building was one of the few intact structures in the City, a squarish, two-storey block with large high-ceilinged rooms on the bottom floor and a honeycomb of square rooms on the second floor.

"Two rules," Raahi said, once the carts were parked and the building was scouted clear. "One, nobody goes anywhere by themselves. No exceptions. Two, don't turn on any taps or toilets or showers in here, anything linked to water. They still work. And they're linked to the Rinse. Break the first rule and it's on your head if something goes wrong. Break the second one and I'll drag you to the Bridge and throw you off into the Rinse myself."

A handful of prefabs were sent to dig new latrines at the back of the building. No one complained. Lien wasn't surprised. Breathing in the City was like having sutures punched across anyone's sense of reality. The air smelled completely different from the Scab. It was sweet and fresh, even over the latrines. Lien had breathed it in greedily the first time she'd come to the City. Now she knew better. Being able to smell nothing but the City meant no warning signals. Meant rations tasted blander than they were. After a day or so it always got disorienting. She was always glad to breathe in the sweat-stink of her own body and the baked rustmetal concrete smell of the Scab whenever she left. There was no wind in the City, and sounds were either dampened or amplified. The sky was a domed shimmer that brightened and darkened to its own beat, encasing the City away from the sun.

Raahi walked over to Lien's side by the carts. "Doesn't look like Serverun got this far," Lien said.

"Oh, he did. Probably went deeper into the City. Didn't see the other two APCs," Raahi said.

"You tell him where to go?"

"No. I told him not to Bridge out of window."

"Think he made it?"

"I didn't think he'd make it this far in the first place. Who knows," Raahi said.

"I don't like the stormsign on the Bridge," Lien said. She looked over into the lobby of the building, where Yusuf and Servertu were settling down in a defensible corner, watching everyone else. "Servertu warned about something he called the Great Change."

"Heard about something like that in Kandan," Raahi said. He spat to the side. "Academics. Did a job for the Kandan University people once. They'd talk your ear off if you give them half the chance. Ask you to fetch Changer-knows-what artefacts for them that don't work. Lot of them think if they can understand how the Change happened they can turn back time. Fix all of this." Raahi waved at the shimmering sky.

"Not a bad dream."

"Me, I'd rather dream about things I can get. I agree, the stormsign isn't good. We'll do a short run. Do what we can in a day and Bridge back in the first stable window."

"Real short." Sup runs usually stayed in the City for a week.

Any longer and even basic equipment like compasses tended to start breaking down. "Your crew going to like that?"

"Probably not, but what happened to Huihui unnerved everybody."

"Did you tell Serverun about safe and dark zones?"

"I told him. Whether he listened…" Raahi trailed off. "Did you tell your Bossman about it?"

"Not really any of your business, is it?"

Raahi raised his hands palms up in mock surrender, turning to check on the carts. Lien walked over to Yusuf and Servertu. They'd chosen a good corner, near a side exit that could lead out to the latrines. The lobby of the safehouse was large, allowing everyone else to cluster near the cook fire by the porch or settle in along the walls. "Raahi doesn't plan on staying long. Just tomorrow, and he wants to leave the day after," Lien told them.

Yusuf nodded. Servertu dug in his saddlebags, handing Lien a taelstick. She glanced at it, checked the balance, and slotted it into her clothes. "Thanks for your time," Servertu said, reaching out with a palm. "I appreciate all that you've done for us."

Lien shook his hand and pocketed the stick. "What are the two of you going to do?"

"Rest here tonight, then head out tomorrow," Servertu said.

"To find the Room?"

Servertu nodded. "If we can."

"Do you even know where it is?"

"I've narrowed it down to a few possibilities."

"If it takes longer than a day to do whatever you want to do, Raahi will leave you behind," Lien warned.

"And you should go with him if you like," Servertu said. He smiled gently. "Don't worry about us."

Lien shook her head. "You *know* I'm coming with the two of you. The photograph is why I even agreed to take you here in the first place." She could admit it to here, under a shimmer-sky, breathing in nowhere air. Taels were one thing, but after seeing the photograph, after hearing Servertu's talk about the worsening Change—after the stormsign on the Bridge—*now* Lien had to know. And besides. With the fortune she was now wearing, she wouldn't be safe around Raahi and the others. Good scout or not. Someone would have seen Servertu hand her the taelstick.

"Trouble?" Yusuf asked, his eyes flicking up towards the carts.

"Everything in the City is trouble," Lien said, "but at least we don't have to worry about Crows here. They don't like the City because they can't fly. Something about the air makes them too heavy."

"What else is in here?" Yusuf gestured at the defensive perimeter that Raahi was setting up with his crew. "Doubt all that security's for fun."

"It's hard to describe. I've never seen what else lives in the City. We don't set up camp further than here, and we stick to the safe zones. Districts like here, where lightsticks, fuel, guns, and such work. Rules of reality are pretty close to actual reality. The dark zones… you'll know them when you see them. Things live in those, we think. Sometimes crew go missing, especially if they walk around alone. But usually, if we respect the City, it's less dangerous than out in the Scab."

"For now," Servertu said. He was flipping through a sketchbook, an older one that he'd fished out from the packs.

"If you know that something is going to happen, I have to tell Raahi," Lien said. Wasn't just out of courtesy or necessity. Deep down, Lien was a firm believer in basic decency. Especially in a place where reality itself was unmoored.

"I don't have enough data to come to a conclusion either way. But if Raahi wants to play it safe, he should Bridge out tomorrow. Tell him that."

"I'll let him know," Lien said, though she knew that wouldn't budge Raahi. Not while they were already in the City. Cutting the run down to a day was already a big concession. Even if Raahi was willing to listen, his crew wouldn't be happy leaving empty-handed.

"I'm disappointed," Raahi said when Lien told him that they were leaving early, "but not surprised. It's why I used to swing by Basa'at to get you even if I didn't have to make the stop. You don't up and leave on a job."

"We won't make trouble for you," Lien promised. "But your people should Bridge out tomorrow."

"You know I can't. The crew will mutiny, if they have to leave empty-handed."

"I thought you'd say that."

"Thanks for the warning. Now, about what we discussed before?"

"I know. I won't stir things up for you with Serverun. I don't want to start a war with an army. Assuming they're still even alive after crossing at high ebb," Lien said.

"I think they probably are. They've got tech like we haven't seen before. Wouldn't be surprised if they had something that made them immune to the Rinse."

"There was that APC on the bridge," Lien said.

"We didn't see the others–they made it through. The Bossman probably kept the best tech for himself."

"I can believe that," Lien said. She looked over to the doorway to the safehouse. Servertu was strapping down the saddlebags, his back turned. Yusuf glanced over though, stiff-backed.

Raahi followed her gaze. "Archivist tech, maybe?"

"Don't know about that."

Raahi sniffed. "I've been thinking. I was wondering how the three of you caught up. We would've seen you coming if you were right on our tail. APCs each had a sniper with a high-powered rifle. One keeping the Crows at a distance, the others were watching our back. They would've seen you and your mounted friend, easy."

"Scab's a big mess. Easy to hide."

"I think the three of you caught up by following the Rinse. But you don't look any different from the last time I saw you."

Lien forced a laugh. "Followed the Rinse? How would we do that and stay UnChanged?"

"That's what I'd like to know." Raahi made a gesture. Prefabs stepped out from behind the supply carts, guns raised. "I'm going to need to take a look in those saddlebags."

"Raahi," Lien said, shocked.

"You don't rob crew in the Scab," Raahi acknowledged, tapping Lien on the shoulder with a finger, "but you're not crew on this run. Sorry, Lien."

"Come on, man. You've already been paid."

"That stormsign on the Bridge isn't like anything I've seen. But I've heard about what happened at Selangor. I think if we want to get out of here, we're going to need what you have," Raahi said.

Lien held up her hands. "We can head out together. How about that? If you people wait here until we're done with the City, we can Bridge back together."

"Sure thing. If you leave whatever tech you've got here. We'll wait a day. You come back in time, we'll all Bridge."

Yusuf was good, but if Raahi's crew opened fire… "Raahi, seriously. This isn't right and you know it," Lien said.

"Be grateful I'm just taking the tech and not your pay." Raahi smiled condescendingly. The urge to punch it off his mouth was close to overwhelming.

"It's fine," Servertu said. "I'm happy to make the exchange. By way of a trade."

Raahi laughed. "Looks like you're the one at my mercy, Archivist. Yeah, I know who you are. Serverun mentioned it."

"Then you know the power behind me. Should it ever be known in the Citadel that you hurt an Archivist, you'd find its doors closed to you and your friends."

The prefabs behind Raahi muttered uneasily. "What kind of trade?" Raahi asked, suspicious.

"Information. You've been travelling with Serverun for days. You'd know how many men he took with him. And where he might be headed."

"Suppose I might." Raahi made another gesture, and his crew relaxed, lowering their guns. "All right. We'll trade. Lien. Go over and take out whatever gear it is. Put it on the floor. Gently."

Lien glared at Raahi. "I'm never working with you again, asshole."

"Maybe you won't have to, if things pan out right for both of us. Move."

Reluctantly, Lien sidled over to Yusuf's flank, cursing herself all the while. She'd been too godsdamned trusting. Shouldn't have accepted Raahi's offer of sanctuary in the first place. Let alone Bridged with him. She should've talked Servertu into losing a day. Furious with herself, she opened the saddlebag that

Servertu indicated. It was stuffed full of strange metallic devices and books. "It's the silver box," Servertu said.

The box was heavy and weirdly cold. Lien grunted as she lifted it out, bracing her weight to do so. "We walk to the gate," Lien told Raahi. "Make the exchange there." Raahi flicked his eyes over the strain she obviously felt from lifting the box and nodded. Lien wouldn't be able to make a quick getaway holding something this heavy.

Once at the gate, Lien set the box on the ground as Raahi's crew backed off. "So how does this work?" Raahi asked.

"It's already switched on." Servertu removed his bangle, tossing it to the ground. Reluctantly, Lien and Yusuf followed suit. "As long as whoever's wearing the bangles stays close to the box, they'd be fine. Your turn."

"Serverun brought twenty-four people. Heavily armed. He asked me for directions to Fusionopolis. When I said I didn't know where that was, he didn't ask me anything else about the City."

If this unnerved Servertu he didn't show it. He inclined his head, nudging his knees against Yusuf's flanks. Lien backed away to the gate with them, unlooping the chains. She was glad that her claws lacked sweat glands. If she'd had UnChanged hands, they would have been clammy from fear and rage. Raahi and the others stared in silence as they let themselves out and ducked out of sight around the brick wall. Yusuf gestured towards a nearby street and broke into a canter. Lien followed, scrambling around cars. Shouts in the compound behind them. An argument was breaking out.

They sprinted three blocks until Lien's lungs felt like they were burning up. Yusuf slowed down in a refuse-choked alley, looking over his shoulder as Lien leaned against the wall, breathing hard. "Clear," Yusuf said.

"I'm so sorry," Lien said.

"Expected worse." Yusuf's tail twitched.

"Worse how? That they'd shoot us on the way out?"

Yusuf eyed Lien frankly. "Thought you'd side with him and *then* shoot us on the way out."

"Yusuf," Servertu chided. He didn't look upset by the

equipment loss. "No matter. It was a good trade."

"Good? We… wait, was that box for something else altogether?" A double-cross would serve Raahi right.

"Oh no. It was for exactly what I said it was. An experimental Archivist machine that stabilises duality around you."

"You have another one?"

"No."

"How is it a good trade then?" Lien demanded.

"It's good to know what we're going to be up against."

"Assuming Raahi was telling the truth." Lien felt depressed all over again. "And Fusionopolis? I don't know where that is either. Which means it's probably not in any of the safe zones."

"APCs should be easy to track. If they made it off that bridge. We'll circle back to one of the main roads, see if we can pick up where they went," Yusuf said.

"We should also find a good place to rest overnight. I don't know any other safehouses out here." Lien pushed down her panic and managed a wan smile. This was a first. She'd never ventured beyond Raahi's network of pre-established safehouses before. Not without a fully-equipped sup run at her back. "If we want to avoid Raahi we'd have to pick a place closer to the dark zones, but I'd rather not chance it."

Yusuf glanced up at the sky. "Still early out. We've got the time."

"All right." This wasn't beyond salvage. Lien looked around. "Let's find a building that I can climb for a better look."

CHAPTER ELEVEN

They found one of the APCs at the edge of a dark zone. A long-barrelled turret sat at the top, overlooking two entry hatches. They were on the northwestern fringe of the safe zone, further than Lien would normally go. The APC had rammed into an overgrown wall surrounding a large field marked with rusted frames on either end. The tiered building beyond was silent and veiled with thick vines that ran riot with pink and white flowers. The air close to the frames pulsed with human-shaped impressions, faceless and chasing a sphere. The single-scented air was broken by an odd sibilant noise that came out of nowhere, the laughter of shadows and ghosts. Lien shivered as she approached the APC noiselessly, peering into the front. The driver was slumped over the wheel. Pink and white flowers grew in a creeping mass out of the stump of their neck, sprawling over the dashboard. There was a rifle slung over the driver's lap, spent shells lying on the empty passenger's seat.

Lien looked back at Yusuf and shook her head. She was about to climb up and check the hatch of the APC when a hollow banging sound reverberated from within, along with a low moan. "Hello?" Lien asked. "Anyone there?"

The moan was cut off. Something scraped and scuttled along the armoured hull of the APC. Yusuf backed off, raising his rifle to cover her as Lien crawled up the APC to the top hatch beneath the turret. "Hello?" Lien rapped lightly on the hatch.

A wet gurgling sound answered her from within. Lien flinched as something banged against the metal flank. Yusuf motioned for her to get clear. As Lien was preparing to jump off, someone whispered, "Hello? Anyone there?"

"Hey. You guys crashed, uh, do you need help?" Lien asked.

Another wet gasp. "Help?"

Yusuf beckoned Lien over urgently. She shook her head. "They sound hurt. I'm going to try and get them out. Maybe if we start up the APC, or carry them back to where Raahi is—"

The hatch slammed open, hard enough to shear it off its hinges. Lien overbalanced with a yell, her jointed limbs scratching uselessly over metal as she fell off the side. Something burst out and lunged through the space she'd been in. It was wet and fleshy, worm-like, with once-human vestigial hands and legs along its flanks, toes and fingers melting together. It swung around, hissing through a long mouth that rolled open along its flank like a zipper. Reddish slime dripped off its extremities as it turned this way and that, tasting the air. Lien pressed a clawed hand over her mouth and forced herself to stay as still as she could. She wouldn't even breathe. Eventually, disappointed, it slid back into the hatch in gleaming coils.

Silence. Lien sucked in a grateful breath. She pulled herself up and backed off, trembling. They gave the APC a wide berth. "What the Changer was *that?*" Lien hissed once they were at a safe distance.

"The soldiers who were in the APC. Accelerated change. That thing was like the creature we saw in the apartment, except even further developed." Servertu spoke with hushed awe. "Maybe that's what happens in the City. Near the City. The end-stage of the mutation. Imagine that. If the mutates could keep combining, gaining more and more mass... *that* could be a reason why your 'dark zones' are unsafe. If there are supermassive organisms in there."

"That's the start of the dark zone?" Yusuf pointed past the walled field. The freshest tracks from the APC led to the road, arcing in past bright yellow plastic marking posts that had been staked into the soil. The City degraded everything but plastic.

Lien was grateful for the change in topic. She didn't want to think of giant worm-creatures being common where they were going. "As of the last time we were here, yes." The first couple of days of a sup run was usually spent resetting all the plastic posts.

"You'd know when we cross into a dark zone. The smell of the air changes. And the plants are different."

"Known risks?" Yusuf asked.

"The Change becomes unstable, that's all we know. Whatever lives in there tends to avoid safe zones. Never seen one." Lien couldn't help looking back over at the APC. "Like I said. Usually, getting to the City is the hard part."

Servertu reached over, pressing his palm to her shoulder. "If you want to turn back, go ahead."

"That stormsign on the Bridge. Do you think this whole area is going to get worse? Including Basa'at?"

"None of this is predictable."

"And you truly think that getting to the Room will help you stop this next 'Great Change' from happening."

"It won't be like turning off a switch, but it'll be a big step," Servertu said.

Lien took in a few steadying breaths. "Okay. Okay. Let's do it."

At the line of yellow posts, Lien wavered. She was now consciously walking away from all that she had been before. Her shop in Basa'at felt like it was stretching away from her, speeding into an unreachable distance. As a scout, Lien had never ventured into a dark zone save to mark its border and retreat. This was the unknown and it should have frightened her more than it did. Her first step wavered, but her next didn't hesitate.

Lien had steeled herself for it, but the humid heat of the dark zone always hit her like a slap in the face. The crisp clean scent of the air faded abruptly into a constant sour stink of rotting refuse. The Scab, baked and compressed in the damp. Behind her, Yusuf's steady clop faltered. He grumbled something unintelligible and pushed on. The City was built in a grid pattern of large thoroughfares bisected by side-streets. Only a few paces behind them, the safe zone was overgrown with lush plants in brilliant colours. The plant life quickly ebbed into stranger forms. Pale lichen covered every surface, even glass, some scaly, some furry. Deeper into the zone, existing plant life looked like it had fused with the buildings themselves. Hybrid trees with corded trunks of wood and concrete sprouted leaves of glass and flesh. Everything was warped into everything else. Stepping into the dark zone felt like walking into a complete entity, a single grotesque sculpture blown huge.

Supermassive organism.

"Lien, to your left," Servertu said. Lien stilled. She backed a step to the side and saw it. Another bubble, slow-growing.

"Maybe you should lead," Lien said weakly. Her gut felt like it was twisting into knots on itself. She could taste something acidic on her tongue. "I'm joking," she said, as Servertu started to dismount. "How do you see it? The bubbles?"

"My eyesight is well-made."

"Funny," Lien said, a little annoyed at the dig.

"I wasn't—" Servertu stopped as Yusuf cleared his throat.

She picked her way over the asphalt, watching for bubbles. The second bubble was huge, swelling over an orange plastic shelter with a warped metal bench. Lien avoided that one easily, looking with passing curiosity at the twisted pole beside it.

"A bus stop," Servertu said. He sounded contrite. "Before the City was abandoned, it was like the Citadel. Or, more accurately, it was a progenitor of the cities we have now."

"No non-essential chatter please," Lien said. She was stressed enough.

"Ah, of course." Servertu subsided.

Past the bus stop, a concrete tiered structure was completely threaded through with trees. Most of the trunks were corded with parts of cars, wooden arteries intertwined with exhaust pipes and engines and seat upholstery. The structure was so thickly overgrown that Lien couldn't make out what was within it. The trees rustled as they passed, leaves angling without a breeze. Sidestepping bubbles on the road, Lien came to the edge of a concrete canal. Once a storm drain, the channel stretched evenly past and around the flank of the tiered building. The water within was a soupy, pulsing mass, a translucent rope of fused water plants, debris, fish. An insectile chitter grew from it as they passed and only subsided once they were a few metres away. Pale spheres of water floated languidly over the channel, drifting from side to side.

Heavy tracks marked the next main intersection. "APCs drove down this way," Lien said, pointing at the pattern of displaced vehicles. "Then one came back and swerved down this road. The one we found."

Yusuf looked down the street. The stormsign bubbles were growing larger. The largest expanded over a line of shophouses, its surface slick against the sun. Within the fused glass and steel of the windows something huge and greyish undulated gently. They skirted the bubble to the next intersection. Servertu pointed at a sign with faded white text. "Fusionopolis," he said.

Lien looked down the street, following the direction of the sign. Three blocks down, the road was swallowed up by dense jungle. Vast trees had fused into buildings and burst through the road, forming a canopy of glittering fragments that refracted light over twisted branches in speckled fragments. No through path. Rising out of the trees in the distance was a pair of glass buildings, connected by delicate bridges. Unlike everything else in the dark zone, they'd been untouched. Something about the gentle curves of the buildings felt familiar.

"I don't like the look of that already," Lien said.

"We're probably headed that way." Yusuf sounded resigned as he drew up beside her.

"Last chance to turn back," Servertu said. He rested one palm on Yusuf's flank and reached over to press the other on Lien's shoulder. Yusuf snorted.

Lien patted Servertu's knuckles with her claw. "If I die—or change into something disgusting—I'm going to come back and haunt the two of you."

"Can try," Yusuf said, and chuckled, the closest Lien had heard him come to a genuine laugh.

"Figures that you'd find our impending horrible deaths funny, halfer."

"We're not dead yet." Yusuf tipped down his hat, squaring his shoulders. "Lead on."

The last APC was idling at the wide steps leading up to the closest glass building. Empty. Lien scanned the forest behind them as Yusuf circled the APC. As forbidding as it had looked, the walk had been uneventful. The forest had been uncomfortably silent, the only noise the clops of Yusuf's hooves and their slow breaths. As Lien studied the road they had emerged from, the trees rustled and shook in the still air. Yusuf flinched with a loud oath. The openings in the forest were narrowing, the structure-trees groaning as they sprouted interlocking thorns and branches. Closing the path.

"That's reassuring." Even Yusuf sounded strained.

"Did Serverun just do something?" Lien asked. She took a laborious breath. This deep in the dark zone, she felt like she was trying to strain air into her lungs through a soup. Everything in the world was taking on a too-sharp focus that started to hurt her eyes.

"Don't think that was him." Yusuf looked over at Servertu for clarification, frowning as Servertu dismounted. "I can fit through those doors."

"I know." Servertu walked up a few steps until he was on eye-level with Yusuf. "Yusuf, you've been by my side since the Citadel. You're the most important person—"

"Hey." Yusuf clasped Servertu's arms. "You're going to have to shoot me to keep me out here." He leaned over, resting his forehead briefly against Servertu's. Stepping back, Yusuf pretended to glower at Lien. "Okay. Show's over."

"Don't I get a speech?" Lien asked lightly. Servertu pulled a face and waved her up the steps. He shook his head as Yusuf tugged him towards the saddle, peering past Lien's shoulder as she cautiously poked her head through shattered glass. The lobby of the building was empty. It was a vast space, ribbed with flat glass planes that sat dark under stripes of dead lights. A lift lobby was at the far end, past a rank of glass gates with security panels that sat dark.

"They came through here," Lien said, pointing at fresh grass and mud stains from sets of heavy boots that led to the gates.

Servertu pushed debris away from a long steel and glass counter by the gates. "Here's a map. This part of the building's mostly admin floors, classrooms, lecture halls, and unrelated laboratories. What we're looking for would be… there. The other building. Restricted access basement level. Bioengineering laboratories."

"So why did Serverun and the others go through here?" Lien

asked.

The reason made itself obvious as they left the building and tried to cross to the second. Bubbles taller than Yusuf were stacked over each other, walling them off from the second building at ground level. Yusuf looked up to the bridges between, tipping back his hat. There was a flicker of movement. Yusuf glanced at Lien, who nodded. "Doesn't look like we can avoid a fight," he told Servertu.

"We don't know how many people he has left," Servertu said, frustrated. "There has to be another way in."

"Huihui. Raahi's scout on the Bridge. The bubble she touched popped," Lien said.

"After her skin stuck to it." Yusuf started to turn around.

"Servertu!" Lien shouted, too late. Servertu had stepped forward, hand outstretched. Lien grabbed him as his fingertips made contact. Servertu went still, squeezing his eyes shut. He didn't budge as Lien tried to pull him free.

"Stop that," Servertu said, without looking up. "Stand back, both of you."

"But—" Yusuf had his hands over Servertu's shoulders.

"Yusuf."

Yusuf let out a hoarse snarl. He backed off a step, stamping his hooves. Lien followed, though she stayed within reach. Her claws twitched against her flanks as Servertu clenched his palm into a fist.

The bubble popped. Breathing hard, Servertu stumbled, flinching as Lien steadied him. "One more," he said, cradling his hand against him. Pulling away before Lien could check the damage, Servertu ducked through the cleared space, touching the next large bubble.

It took longer to burst. Servertu staggered through once it was done, falling on his knees in the long grass and clutching his wrist. Lien scuttled through. She grabbed Servertu's wrist and turned up his palm, ignoring his murmured protests—and gawked.

"Your hand. It's prefab." The skin had been flayed away, but the blistered skin was beading up with pale fluid instead of blood. Lien had never seen prefab human parts look or feel this real. There was usually something oddly glossy or clumsy about them that even mediocre creature parts lacked. The human eye was quicker to pick out flaws in human parts, perhaps. Whatever reason it was, human-appearing parts weren't popular in these parts.

Servertu pulled his hand away. "I'm prefab," he said, getting unsteadily to his feet. He had to be steadied by Yusuf, who curled an arm protectively around the small of Servertu's back.

"That's why you're UnChanged," Lien said. She looked Servertu over with a new light. "It's great work. I've never seen human prefab parts look so good."

"Because none of it is a graft. I'm completely prefab. Other than my brain." Servertu tapped his temple. "It's the reason I'm here. The image I gave you is a copy of a drawing I made in the Archives. Photorealistic. I've seen it too." Servertu hesitated. "More accurately, I'm not sure if I've seen it. I know I have the memory of it."

Lien took out the colourstat. Now that she looked closely, what she had thought were grainy scratches and dust speckles on the small picture were lines from a pen. The image was too faded for her to tell. Servertu showed her his sketchbook from within his robes. On the last page, the Bridge had been rendered in precise lines. Even drawn in a rush, it looked ready to touch.

"I'm not prefab," Lien said. She waved her claws in limp assertion.

"You're not prefab. Nor were the others I found."

"Where did you... was it Yaran? Where your parts were made?"

"Where I was made?" Servertu corrected. His mouth had compressed into a thin line. "No. I don't know. I woke up fully formed in the Archives. A delivery to be studied, at least at first. The Archivists grew fond of me. The subject of study became one of those who studied. Yet something was always missing."

"What was it?"

Servertu looked human. Under her stare, Servertu looked away. He wrapped his raw palm from bandages in the saddlebags. "I'm functional but incomplete. Much of the human experience is a learned response, but I don't think it's *all* meant to be learned."

"You're here to, what, find out how to be human?" Lien asked, incredulous. "Changer, you look more human than I do. There's no longer a standard for 'human,' especially not out here. Good riddance to all that." .

Servertu was already shaking his head. "I know what I am and what I'm not. I accept it." He stroked Yusuf's flank, making the halfer prance and snort. "I'm here to understand why. The reason I was made, the reason why we remember this Room. I do think it's key to understanding the Change."

"What about Serverun?" Lien asked. "If you're called 'Servertu' and he's called—"

"Talking about people behind their backs?"

The disembodied, electronically burred voice had floated down out of nowhere. Lien flinched back a step, bringing up her daggers. Yusuf stepped forward in front of Servertu, aiming his rifle up at the glass doors of the second building. Servertu narrowed his eyes, pressing a palm against Yusuf's flank. "Serverun."

"Since you're all here, you might as well come in." The glass doors slid open with a grinding sound, rattling along hidden grooves. "There's a fire escape that'll lead to the lower floor after the second left. See you soon." There was a harsh click.

"I hate traps," Lien said into the silence. "Just making that clear."

CHAPTER TWELVE

Nothing exploded in the lobby. Unlike the main building, this building's lobby had no security gates and no desk. Large glass panels hung from the ceiling on thin silver cabling. The closest panel lit up as Lien got too close. Flinching back, she nearly collided with Yusuf. Servertu sidestepped them both, studying the images and text that flicked up. There was a large map and smaller images of creatures Lien didn't recognise.

"Chernobyl," Servertu said. At their blank expression, he explained, "A disaster from a long time ago. Before the wars. The people evacuated, but the animals were left to run wild in an exclusion zone. Some of them adapted to the radiation." He walked to the next screen, which lit up in dense data beside an image of a winding spiral. "It says here that Fusionopolis decided to dedicate its life sciences division towards studying their mutation. Finding a way to replicate it on a large scale."

Yusuf jerked to the side as a panel beside him lit up. It showed an illustration of a man impressed against a perfect circle, dissected into jigsaw parts of changeable pieces. "Prefab technology," Yusuf said. He prodded the illustration with a finger, leaving a blip of light. "I've seen this drawing in Yaran. Much bigger, carved over the door of the Central Fabrix."

"I'm not exactly comfortable staying here to study ancient technology while there's a kill team possibly all around us," Lien muttered. They were exposed out here.

"I've been listening for trouble," Yusuf said.

"Not saying you haven't. Just thinking there's a lot of dark corners for someone with a high powered rifle."

"If Serverun wanted to snipe us he would've done it from high ground while we were on our way here. I checked. No windows were broken," Yusuf said. He did, however, scan the exits again.

Thankfully, the rest of the panels stayed quiet. Damaged, maybe. The corridors looked empty. Overhead lights blinked on as they took the second left. Lien flinched, then covered her nervousness with a laugh. "Nevermind your taels, if I could haul out whatever's still running power through this place, I could buy Basa'at."

Yusuf sniffed. He covered her as Lien checked the fire escape. Clear. The stairs down were dark, but at least the stairwell was wide enough to fit Yusuf and Lien apace. "So this Serverun guy. Rival Archivist?" Lien asked.

"Not particularly," Servertu said. He looked visibly uncomfortable. "It's difficult to explain. Better that you see it."

"Does he want to kill you?"

"If he did, he would've stationed snipers on the upper floors. Like Yusuf said."

"Maybe he didn't have people to spare." The worm in the APC they had found, Changer.

The reminder sobered Servertu up. He was quiet as Lien made her way as quietly as she could down to the basement floor. The door was closed. Unlocked. Lien started to ease it open, only to leap back with drawn daggers as something hauled it wide. The person who had opened the door was Servertu's height, dressed in grey fatigues with a black enclosed helmet over his head. They glanced at Servertu, then at Yusuf.

"Serverun," Servertu said.

Serverun pressed something against the base of his helmet. The opaque metal and glass pulled away in folding leaves, earthing down over his collar. Lien stifled a gasp. It was Servertu. An identical twin? Even the hair was the same. Serverun stared at her with a disapproving frown, turning to lope away down the corridor without asking them to follow.

Servertu jogged up beside him. "Where are your soldiers?"

"Unstable Change on the upper floors. Caught us by surprise."

"Dead?"

Serverun's lip curled. "Not precisely."

Lien shivered.

"Then you're too late. Give up," Servertu said gently.

"I'm not about to stand by and let you unmake us," Severun said.

"That's not what I'm here to do."

"You might have enough curiosity for the both of us but I have pragmatism. Stand aside."

"Why are you helping me then?" Servertu asked.

"I'm not." Serverun glanced over his shoulder at Lien. "You know it's too late for you. Your Change. Don't you feel it? You aggravated it by coming into the dark zone. No Injunct can help you now."

"Your point being?" Lien asked, even as her heart dropped into her stomach. She wasn't going to give him the satisfaction.

Serverun frowned at her. "You don't know why Servertu brought you here? That's rich."

"He didn't bring me here. I brought myself. He only asked me to bring him to the City."

"He gave you the colourstat, didn't he. Why would he do that? He could have easily doubled whatever he's paying you instead. Offered enough for you to come here without giving you something like that. But that would've made you suspicious. You might have said no. So he pushed only enough to make it look like he wasn't pushing. Servertu's smart—if you haven't seen that by now, I don't have much hope for you."

Lien stared hard at Servertu, whose eyes were averted. "So why am I here?"

"You have to see the Room," Servertu said. His shoulders were hunched, as though in shame.

Lien stopped walking. "I'm not moving another step until you give me an explanation."

Servertu turned. His face was bleak. He shook his head at Yusuf as Yusuf's grip tightened on his rifle, and Yusuf stepped away with a brief look of relief. "You will," Servertu said, with an inexorable gentleness. "Better that you keep walking now. Before you Change the rest of the way and have no choice. It's up to you."

"What do you mean I'll have no choice?"

"The City is a single vast organism. Once you Change, you'd become part of it. Part of the Room. Had you stayed in Basa'at, eventually you would have turned ghulkin and come to the City. Come now, while it's still a controlled decision."

When Lien couldn't answer, Servertu kept walking. Serverun frowned at Lien. He looked as though he wanted to say something more, but swallowed it and jogged to keep up.

"Yusuf," Lien said, uncertain.

Yusuf stared at her. Lien wasn't sure what she'd wanted to see. Sympathy? Only moments ago Yusuf had clearly been prepared to threaten her to keep walking. And yet there it was. Guarded pity. Seeing it pissed her off. Lien grit her teeth, her claws curling in the air. Yusuf tipped his hat at her and kept walking, his hooves ringing echoes down the sterile grey corridors.

Lien folded her legs beneath her and sat down. At the far end of the corridor, the others turned a corner. Soon even the sound of Yusuf's hooves faded away. Once alone, Lien closed her eyes. She wasn't sure how long she sat, listening to nothing. At the end of nothing, Lien pulled up her tunic. She let out a hoarse groan. The striated tissue that fed up from her waist had spread up to her breasts. Tiny hard knobs were pushing out from the greyish-pink flesh, contracting as they came in contact with the air. Pain pulsed through her spine and through her thorax in a dull ache, followed by a wet roiling feeling, something coming free within her. Lien scrambled up and took a step back. She'd left a dark bluish stain on the metal floor that smelled of turpentine.

Nowhere to go. Lien imagined leaving, retreating into the City. Finding Raahi. Raahi was an asshole, but he would do for her what she had done for Cheung. She'd be able to count on him to bury her, if only because her corpse would attract scavengers to his camp. If she died, would she still be part of the City? Part of the Scab? Servertu's words were the truth. Nothing tended to hurt as much as the truth.

Angrily, Lien pulled her shirt back down. The first step she took felt like she was forcing something forward that was only tenuously attached to her body. It was a frightening feeling at first, then a freeing one. One leg already almost wasn't hers. Was this how worms were made on the dark face of the world? A slow relinquishment of autonomy until only resentment remained? Lien bared her teeth and kept walking. Down the corridor.

The next corridor fed through several dark rooms to a blast door at the far end, where Yusuf was waiting. He didn't look surprised as she hobbled painfully over, nor did he approach her to help. Bastard. He stayed quiet while Lien cursed him with each step. She was gasping by the time she was close enough to realize why Yusuf hadn't even flicked his tail once on her long walk over. His eyes were wide, fixed into the distance, hands loose at his flanks.

"Yusuf?" Lien hobbled over. Two of her legs and her vestigial limbs weren't responding well now. It was getting more difficult to breathe, the air growing heavier. More humid. She pressed a claw tentatively against his flank, which left another turpentine stain. Yusuf didn't flinch. His hands relaxed over his rifle, and it began to slide slowly out of his grip. Lien could take the hint, if that was what it was. She took the rifle from him, cradling it awkwardly.

The blast doors opened once Lien was in arm's reach. The chamber within looked nothing like the colourstat. It was thick with corruption. The steel and glass cabinets, gurneys, and consoles within had long fused into thick stems that connected the sides of the Room in every direction. The console screens flicked on as she stepped closer, pale rectangles of light in the gloom. The air was a faint tracery of filament-like roots translucent to the eye and gritty against Lien's skin. Air itself, cycling into the Change. Was this what the Great Change was like? Air becoming like earth, earth to air? Lien tightened what was left of her claws around the rifle and forced herself through. The filaments caressed her face and shoulders with a grotesque maternal familiarity. She breathed them in to tickle her throat. On her tongue, the filaments weren't liquid, gaseous, or solid, but something in between, a fourth state that existed in the broken lines of reality.

Lien reached the closest console screen. She pressed the tip of a claw to it and was unsurprised to watch her hand sink through. The yield was reluctant. As Lien pulled her hand back up, part of her claw was missing, the stump capped in spikes of silver and glass. Too late for panic. Lien walked on. The Room felt hot, then cold. Something loosened under her shirt and tumbled to the floor. One of the vestigial limbs. The wet patch that spread against her clothes smelled like a Crow's charnel breath.

The centre of the Room was warm and alive. Lien couldn't help but think of it as a womb, held in shape on all sides by translucent roots. Within were curled shapes, hands clasped. Lien touched what was left of her claw to its membrane and was tugged within. The filament-fluid-air was richer within. Lien tried to force her way closer to the shapes, but she was losing mobility. Strands of her hair and clothes floated away against her. A chunk of metal that was Yusuf's rifle. She knew. She had been here before. She had died here and been reborn.

Here was where duality had given way to a third Other. There had been more than six of them, but only six survived. They had all been children of the war, their parents missing or dead. Many of their foster parents hadn't cared to report them missing. Floating, Lien's knees pressed against the remnants of a small chair with fragmenting straps. Hers. A cradle for a small skull had once dangled over the chair. In an attempt to calculate a world out of the end of civilisation, Fusionopolis had tried to create the most powerful artificial intelligence ever made. A technological singularity, one with six organic servers.

"You remember." The speaker was Serverun and Servertu both.

"Not all of it," Lien said. She sank down towards the chair. "We made you."

"You made everything. Instead of forcing a controlled mutation of six people there was a duality breach. The paradox within everything was forced out of balance and made to unwind. The first Great Change."

"And the next? Why is another Great Change happening?"

"This one believes it is a matter of the tides." That sounded more like Serverun. "We were born here. The first prefab human. The first creature to exist without duality."

"What about now?" It was harder to focus. Lien closed with the two shapes now. She had thought their hands clasped. On closer inspection that wasn't the case. Serverun and Servertu's hands were fused together, their fingers melted away. They were absorbing each other.

No one answered. Lien flowed closer yet. Serverun and Servertu were locked in combat, silent as they were. Trying to form into a single entity, its duality paradox back in place, but with a single dominant consciousness. Their closed eyelids fluttered, their faces frozen into frowns. Lien pushed her remaining claw onto their fused hands. She would have bared her teeth if she had any left. Against her, Servertu trembled. The dual paradox, threatened again. Yet he had been waiting for her. Lien's claw melted easily into his wrist as the womb-space contracted. Something rumbled overhead, the building itself quaking at the strain, the womb-creature around them starting to pulse and keen, the pitch rising, rising until it was a child's birthing-cry, the same wailing sound of indeterminate grief and rage that the Crow had made. Serverun's mouth opened wide in a scream that the womb-fluid swallowed. Servertu had wanted to be more. Serverun had only wanted to be whole. The act of Creation was always also an act of necessary violence.

Together Servertu and Lien re-folded fractured duality. She found the safer spaces in between; he flattened and filed down the edges, drawing everything inwards and inwards. First the Room. The forest of steel. The dark zone. The City, the Scab. They pulled every broken fusing into a brilliant snarl of yielding matter, crushing it into something new.

EPILOGUE

Outside the Scab, Yusuf paused as fingertips pressed against his flank. His passenger turned to study the ruin, shading their eyes with a slender palm. Not for the first time since Yusuf had charged into the Room, he wished there was something—someone—he recognised in their face. There was something of Lien in the colour of their skin and their dark hair, their easy poise. Something of Servertu in the slope of their shoulders. Nothing else. They were wrapped in scavenged clothes. Servertu's sketchbooks, Serverun's helmet, and Lien's daggers were stowed in Yusuf's saddlebags.

"The Crows will start to die off," his passenger said. Their voice sounded closest to Lien's.

"Now that they're too heavy to fly?"

The passenger nodded. "The ghulkin will thrive. Maybe the psychons. Without hot Change over the Rinse, Raahi should be able to get out easily."

"Curse that guy," Yusuf said. He held grudges.

The passenger patted Yusuf's flank absently, the way Servertu used to. That hurt. Yusuf turned his face away and pulled down his hat, hoping to hide his heartsickness. The passenger exhaled. "Yusuf."

"What do I even call you now?" Yusuf winced at the rawness in his voice.

"What would you like to call me?"

Servertu had asked the same question a long time ago when Yusuf had first met him in the Citadel. Within the Archives he had been Server Two. Calling him Servertu had originally been a joke, a cruel one that Yusuf had later come to regret. Even if Servertu had been indifferent to it.

"You pick," Yusuf said.

There was a pause. "I'll think about it."

"Where now?"

"Selangor. We did something to the Change. It might not have been enough. We should check. See if the storm has moved on."

"All right." Yusuf started towards the distant slopes. Even the air smelled different now. Cleaner. They could rest in Basa'at. Head out from there. "Is it all going to get better? The world. Return to what it was?"

"There's no utopia to return to. The world's been moving towards this end for a long time. It grew too warm, too quickly. The final extinction event ended years before the Last Summer. All I've done is slow the descent. Given civilization a temporary reprieve."

"So what was the point?"

"Sometimes a reprieve is all the time we need," the passenger said. They stroked Yusuf's flank as Yusuf bit his retort back down, swallowing his anger, his grief.

With empty hands, Yusuf began to walk.

About the Author

Born in Singapore, Anya moved to Melbourne to practice law, and now works in advertising. Her short stories have appeared in venues such as Strange Horizons, Uncanny, and Daily SF. She can be found on twitter @anyasy and otherwise at www.anyasy.com.

About the Press

Neon Hemlock is an emerging purveyor of queer chapbooks and speculative fiction. Learn more at www.neonhemlock.com and on Twitter at @neonhemlock.